SCARS
and Other Stories

LEE FREDERICK

Published by:
Lee Frederick
MILWAUKEE, WISCONSIN

ISBN-13: 979-8-218-45032-8

Editing: Carol Killman Rosenberg

Interior & cover design: Gary A. Rosenberg

Printed in the United States of America

Contents

To Ericka, Ali and Austin

Acknowledgements

Thanks to my friend Tom Robbins, who has been like Tonto, sending me messages from the other side of the mountain.

Likewise, to the three felons in my life (they know who they are) who educated me more than they know.

Finally, thanks to Tom Newman, my favorite River Rat, who challenged me to tell these stories.

Scars

I was ten when my mother decided that a twenty-foot rope and a tree would babysit me for the summer. The night before the first drop-off, she told me to get my fishing gear and worms ready because she would be taking me to a place where I could fish all day.

"Where?" I asked.

"Somewhere you've never been. I'll make you a sack lunch."

She was a woman who matter-of-factly gave orders, seldom explained why, and never waited around for more discussion.

The next morning, she drove me to the Scott County pump station, a twenty-minute ride from our house in Bluffs. The sign entering our town on Illinois Route 100 read 950, which everyone knew meant population. We had taken the highway south out of town, turned west on a dirt road just after the Oxville bridge, and headed west toward the county's most expensive farming land, called the Bottoms, and the Illinois River.

She parked on top of the bank of the main drainage ditch that fed directly into the pump station's intake pipe. She tied one end of the rope to the tree next to where the car was parked and then walked the rope down to the edge of the bank. She motioned to me to follow her. There she tied the other end of the rope tightly around my waist with a bowline knot in the back.

Satisfied with her work, she said, "Get your stuff out of the car. Here is some lunch and Kool-Aid in the thermos. I prefer you stay out here and fend for yourself rather than running around town like a chicken with your head cut off. I'm going to try to sell some green encyclopedias in Winchester, and I'll be back around four."

The tree was ten yards down the bank from the car, the rope exactly the right length to the bank. I guessed she had already been there and measured the distances; she wouldn't leave that kind of thing to chance.

I stood on the steep bank looking up as she drove off over the horizon. Left alone in this new place, I was scared as hell. I had been thinking for a while that her main goal in life was to make me uncomfortable—at least she had my risk of drowning covered. She was that kind of woman.

My parents had moved to Bluffs in 1946 when I was three, so my father could work at the CIPS utility plant in Meredosia, seven miles away. He died of leukemia within the year, and my mother was left on her own to provide for my thirteen-year-old sister and me. I have no memories of my father.

My mother was a talented woman who got stuck living in a rural village without relatives nearby to lend emotional or financial support. She could care less that the townspeople would use "She's not from around here" as a way of putting her in the lower class. They had learned quickly to stay out of her way or be confronted by a proud woman who was smarter and meaner than they were.

There was this one thing she could do, though, that no one else in the county could. She was an accomplished smocker.

She would sew small dresses for the newborn babies in town and then hand stitch the smock designs on them.

She gave the dresses as gifts, and they would become keepsakes for life in the babies' families. No one else in the area could smock, and it softened her reputation, at least with the village women.

She got a job as a non-degreed, elementary school teacher in Meredosia, where her nine-month salary in 1954 was $1900. To make ends meet for the three of us, she also sold Modern Woodmen Insurance from 1949 to 1952 and then began to sell the *Lincoln Library of Essential Information* in 1953. She filled the back trunk of our 1948 Chevrolet with the green, two-volume sets she sold for a "good commission."

Like all children in those times, we kids were free-range chickens in the summer and totally responsible for our activities. We never asked permission to do anything, we just did it while our parents lived their lives. The only rule we had, and it was a soft one, was to get home for supper. If we didn't make it, no supper.

I had fished often at Vortman's and Korty's ponds and Hammond's creek, usually with my neighbor Herm who was two years older than me. These were bicycle rides out of town with poles across our handlebars and cans of worms in our baskets. Often, we'd go and return with nothing to show for our three-hour expedition. Sometimes we wouldn't even get one bite. Then the next time, we'd catch something big enough to eat and, occasionally, a whopper to brag about. We fished a lot, used the word "luck" a lot. We were never bored.

But at the beginning of this particular summer in 1953, my sister, Janet, who was fourteen, and my mother were not getting along. Janet escaped three hours south on a

Greyhound bus to Tamaroa to stay with our grandmother, our mom's mother. My mother was glad she left. With both children occupied, she was free to drive to nearby towns and sell the *Lincoln Library* sets.

She was an aggressive woman who was not afraid or ashamed to knock on any door and tell people why they needed to buy her encyclopedia. She kept busy and was not going to live her life through her two children.

She was not afraid to tell a neighbor that he parked too close to her spot. "Move your damn car out of our parking place in front of the house," she would yell at them.

This bold behavior made her a *hustler* to the village men, and she scared them. Contrast their fear with the endearment the women felt for her genius at smocking and there you would find me, navigating somewhere in between.

I couldn't sleep the night before the first drop-off because I didn't know what time she would be leaving. My world was centered on my beloved hero, Jackie Robinson, and the Brooklyn Dodgers. Each morning I would get up at 7 a.m. and bicycle to where the wired stack of the *Illinois State Journals* was dropped off in front of the Coffee Cup Café.

I would lift one copy out of the wired stack, take it to the steps of Faye Main's barbershop, check the scores from the night before, then leave it inside the shop's screen door. Faye approved of my reading his newspaper, even though, like everyone else in town, he was a St. Louis Cardinal fan.

He always told me he was charging double when he cut my hair because I was the only Dodger fan in the county. "How can you root for a bunch of Negros," he would whisper in my ear. But inside my heart, I knew he was kidding, because how could anyone not believe that Number 42 wasn't the best player in the world!

The night before drop-off, Preacher Roe had won his fifth game of the season and Jackie had gotten two hits. This good news made me feel better, and I was happy I got to check the box score before we left.

I had never been to the pump station before, but I had heard stories about it. It was where the Barnett and Freesen brothers caught the biggest catfish and carp around. It was considered off-limits for young boys because "there were too many snapping turtles in the water, and the fish were so big they would drag a boy into the water." At least that's what Fred Barnett always said.

I was there all by myself at the Bottoms' pump house; the Illinois River was just over the levee and there was not another person within five miles as far as I knew. Trying to avoid the noticeable pounding in my heart, I quickly put red worms on the hooks of my two bamboo telescopic poles and dropped them in the water, one tight line, the other with a bobber. I sat on the bank, waited for lady luck to visit, and surveyed my summer sitter.

There was the pump house itself, with the metal grate over the intake pipe. The main ditch, where I was located, widened significantly as it entered the grate area. The station was famous for having the biggest internal combustion engine in Scott County.

There was a concrete platform between the grate and the front of the station that I could jump onto, cross, and get to the other side of the main ditch. The tree, rope, and I were on the northeast side of the levee. The Illinois River was west, over on the other side of the levee. I could see two dirt paths going up the levee on both sides of the station that would give me access to the river.

The Bottoms was the most fertile land in the world—at

least that is what we were told. It was flat, rich, black dirt that always produced more bushels per acre of corn than "anywhere else in the world." Many of my fourth-grade classmates lived down here because their fathers were tenant laborers for the rich landowners. Part of their pay was a free house on the farmer's land. My mother always told me that these people "had dirt in their blood."

The problem was this land along the Illinois River was low and vulnerable to flooding on the east side of the levee in the summer, when the corn and soybeans were growing. The drainage districts were created by the rich farmers who built levees and pump houses to suck the heavy summer rains from the east side over to the river side to keep their fields from flooding.

First, I needed to set myself free. I walked up the bank and saw that my mother had tied the one-inch-thick rope to the tree with a slipknot and clove hitch combination. I assumed the same would be at the back waist. I smiled as I returned to my tackle box and got my small buck knife. I wiggled the knot to my front, stuck the dull end into the knot, and pried. Because it was so thick, it came loose quickly, and I stepped out of the loop.

I was afraid of my mother because she would slap me when she was angry. It happened often. I had hit one hundred pounds that winter, but she weighed at least 140 and didn't hesitate to smack me around. She was never a happy woman except a day or two after Ray visited from St. Louis and they "huffed and puffed" downstairs. Janet would report on these events, but I had no idea what she was talking about.

Now that I was over my initial deer-in-the-headlight moments, I was careful to mark the place where the knot began so I could tie myself back up the way she had. I wanted her to trust her system so I could keep coming to this amazing place.

Albeit unconscious, it was my introduction to one of life's reoccurring conflicts, freedom or obedience. Freedom came naturally. I was fishing where only the men could, and I was away from her for the day.

Not feeling guilty, I looked closely at my fishing possibilities. I had a reputation for being a good fisherman "for my age." I knew how to catch crawdaddies, remove their tails, and use them for bait. I caught suckers and carved them for bait. I could clean bluegill and catfish. The quality of my worm supply was well known in town; I kept my night crawlers separate from my garden worms. I fed them with coffee grounds from our neighbors.

I moved my poles closer to the grate over the intake tube and quickly caught two yellow belly catfish, both keepers. I knew that bringing home fish to eat would impress my mother and put her at ease that her plan was working. Next, I moved over the concrete platform and put my poles into the middle of the ditch. I was fishing tight line, and I could tell the water there was the deepest so far. I caught another catfish bigger than the first two and then a big carp that weighed more than the three combined. Neither had pulled me into the water, so I began to wonder if Fred had been exaggerating.

I now had four fish on my stringer that I kept in the water so they would stay alive as long as possible. With the sun directly overhead, the fish stopped biting. I retrieved my sack lunch, returned to the platform, and finished my pickle loaf sandwich and chips quickly, with my back on the east wall of the station. I had already drunk half the Kool-Aid, and I knew I had to stretch out what was left until later in the afternoon.

I was tired from all the excitement that I had experienced since arriving that morning. I leaned back against the brick wall and looked straight east down the main ditch. Two smaller channels from the south entered the main ditch. The possibilities excited the free-range chicken in me.

I knew the fish would not be biting while the sun was high, so I took my bait out of the water and jumped across the gap between the opposite bank and the platform. This was another new world for me. I could see the tree, my rope, and the horizon on the other side. I walked east to the first channel that emptied into the main ditch. With branches and fallen trees in the water, it looked like a great place to fish.

Then I saw it for the first time. A large technicolor snake had slithered into the water on the other side of the channel and began to swim toward me. It scared the shit out of me. I stepped back from the bank, watched it for a few seconds more, and took off for the safety of the station platform. I ran like Jackie Robinson stealing second base.

I had had plenty of experiences on land with blue racers, black, garter, and bull snakes around our town. They were common and not threatening. This one was a monster, like the ones I had seen pictures of in the *Lincoln Library* we had at home.

I caught my breath slowly and then watched a racoon and six babies walk from that south bank down to the water and calmly drink. The mother looked up at me, I was at most twenty yards away, and then she carried on. It was as if she did not see me or at least care that I was there. According to my trusty Timex watch, it was after 3 o'clock then, and I started to get nervous about having enough time to get back into the rope jail.

I returned, tied her knot, and waited for the dust cloud

announcing her return down the dirt road. She arrived before 4 o'clock and was impressed with my catch. She had sold two sets in Winchester and made twenty dollars.

Driving back to town, she said, "So you are okay fishing at the pump station for the summer? It won't be every day, only when I have appointments out of town."

With the wind hitting my face perfectly from the wing window, I looked at her: "Sure. It's a lot better than Vortman's pond."

"That I tie you to the tree is for your safety," she added. "No need to tell anyone in town."

That was that. The deal was made, and, in her way of thinking, she had had the discussion with me.

I fished at the pump station several times before the Fourth of July. I got so I could predict when the racoons would come for a drink. On the other side opossums and skunks would come, muskrats would troll the water next to the banks at different times, and that big snake from the other channel would cross in the middle of the afternoon. Unlike the smaller animals, deer would come to the bank and stare at me for a while, but they would never come to the water and drink.

Everything was going smoothly in my paradise until the snapping turtles figured out that I was a regular visitor and an easy mark for a free meal. As soon as I started filling my stringer, they would swim under water and start feasting on my fish. I swear they would wait for me to arrive, wish me good luck, and get their knives and forks ready.

River snapping turtles are nasty creatures with criminal reputations; they prefer shallow water. The pump station's ditches were no more than five feet deep. I had heard stories about them, like once they bite you, they don't let go until they hear thunder. They are ugly, with snouts that hiss, and can weigh more than twenty pounds. I had to figure out a way to prevent them from eating what I caught.

I had already hooked three of them—actually they had hooked themselves by taking my bait—but they were so big that I couldn't pull them out of the water. They had swallowed the hook, so I had to cut the line and away they swam with a hook in their mouths or throats. I was hoping word would get around in there to stop eating my fish.

I didn't know what to do about them, so I decided to ask Drag Bridgman for advice, the only guy in Bluffs who cleaned snapping turtles and ate them. Drag lived on the corner of my street.

Every small village has its characters known for their odd tastes. Fred Northcutt would eat all the chicken gizzards you would give him. Ted Jarvis preferred rocky mountain oysters to any other food. Drag Bridgman was the snapping turtle guy. When they were available, he would butcher them outside in front of anyone who wanted to watch, usually us boys. It was always a gory mess.

I knew he liked me, so I asked him.

He laughed. "You're a kid—hell men have a hard time killing them. Wait, where have you been seeing them?"

I told him.

"Okay, tie a long rope to your stringer and drop it behind the grate. Turtles can't get back there."

I asked, "But how do the men kill the ones they bring to you?"

"Some of the bigger guys use a hatchet, some shoot them in the head. You know, Billy, you've seen me clean them, they still twitch and move for ten hours or more without their heads."

Including the July Fourth holiday, I didn't return to the pump station until a couple of weeks later. It had been a rough period with my mother. I had asked her what the box labeled Kotex was with all those things with blood on them. Her closet always smelled funny. She grabbed my shirt, pinned me to the wall, then slapped and punched me. "Don't ever go in my closet again," she said.

Then, when the new Baptist minister was visiting in our house, I was lying on the floor and farted in front of him. I didn't know enough to be embarrassed, but I could see my mother was. The minute he walked out the door, she began kicking me with her heavy shoes. I have never farted in public since.

So, I was more than ready to get out of the house and return to my paradise.

I had been thinking a lot about surprising Drag, and I knew he would pay big money. And I needed the peace and quiet of the pump station.

I made a plan. First, I went to Hiermann's Gamble store in town and bought a wire leader and a smaller treble hook. I bought twenty feet of quarter-inch rope, just small enough to tie into the eye of the leader. My idea was to bait the hook with a sucker and use the rope around a tree like a pulley. My pole was just too weak and unhandy. How to kill the snapping turtle was the problem.

Drag had told me that you can't shoot them just anywhere, it had to be in the head to kill the brain. I had a 22 single-shot rifle, all of us boys had one, so I figured I would have to do it that way. First, I had to ask my mother to let me take my rifle on the next trip. I told her how the turtles were taking our food, that Drag had told me how to do it, and he would pay me if I brought him one. To be honest, Drag hadn't said all of that.

Based on the agreement we had made for the summer, she was not all that into overthinking my safety. She was busy doing her own thing. She only said, "Just don't shoot yourself."

"I haven't so far, Mom."

End of the discussion.

I was damn excited to go the next morning and, I must admit, scared. My imagination had me knocking on Drag's door and presenting him with a snapping turtle. Plus the Dodgers had beat the Phillies the night before and Number 42 had gotten the game-winning hit.

I caught a sucker quickly. Next, I slit its belly and shoved the treble hook up toward its mouth. I knew where the turtles hung out, so I put the bait into the water and the rope around the nearest tree. I put a round in my 22 but not in the magazine . . . and waited.

It wasn't long before I could see something stirring in the water. I had made a slipknot loop on the end of my rope to help me pull harder, so I began to slowly put tension on the hook. I could feel something plenty heavy on the line and could feel my heart start to pound. A little more pressure and an ancient dinosaur waddled out of the water toward me. I had not thought out this next part at all.

I guess I thought we would play tug-of-war where I would get a clear head shot. Instead, with a treble hook somewhere in his throat, he headed toward me, hissing all the time. I panicked and escaped up the bank. I looked to see if I could see my heart beating through my sweaty shirt. As I was catching my breath, he turned and waddled back toward the water, so I slid down and grabbed the rope so at least I had hold of him.

I realized then to get a head shot, I would have to have

both hands free. I decided that I would have to hang it some-how, make it secure, and then get my shot. However, suddenly I felt dizzy and tired. It was 12:30, I hadn't eaten or drunk anything, so I went into the shade where I kept my lunch and tried to decide what to do next. I drank all my Kool-Aid in one swallow while my hands and knees shook.

Meanwhile the turtle was yanking and hissing, trying to get loose of the rope I had tied to the tree. He kept trying to get back in the water, but I had shortened the rope so he couldn't. I was watching him closely in case he should decide to charge up the bank and attack me. I forgot about eating and concentrated on saving my life.

I decided I would have to use the bigger tree that my jail rope was tied to because it had a horizontal limb I could use to hang it from. Next, I brought my rifle up to where I thought I could get to it quickly. Taking some deep breaths, I began to pull the turtle up the bank. It was one angry son of a bitch and weighed at least twenty pounds. It hissed and writhed with every pull and was so heavy I could barely get it up the hill.

I finally got enough slack to put the rope around the tree and on top of the horizontal limb, which was about three feet high. I was sitting on the ground pulling and getting him closer. I moved to the other side of the tree and decided where I would secure the rope once I got the turtle to a hanging position. Finally, there, oh, he was angry, I grabbed my rifle, bolted the round in the magazine, moved to a safe position, shot—and missed his head completely because my hands were shaking so much.

My other bullets were in my tackle box, so I ran down and put five in my pocket. My hunting mentors had always advised to give the animal a fair chance. I thought about them as I bolted the round into the magazine. Not into fair at that moment, I put the rifle two inches close to his head and blew it off.

Most of the head was gone, but apparently the hook was further down into his stomach, and the turtle hung there writhing and twisting on the rope. I had no idea what to do next.

It was 2:30, and I never knew exactly when my mother would show up. I guessed I had about an hour of freedom left. I knew I had to get it to bleed out, and to do that, I had to get the neck cavity to face down. It had already splattered blood all over the rope and my jeans, short sleeve shirt, and shoes. There was also plenty of the sticky stuff on my arms and hands.

I took the remaining slack from my hang rope, cut ten feet, and made a slipknot. Then I went to the turtle, made the loop so I could catch its left back claw, pulled it tight, turned it upside down, and cloved it to the same branch. It suddenly convulsed, and the other foot's claw caught my neck. Now I was pissed. And bleeding. I stepped back and once again that day, I looked to make sure my heart wasn't jumping out of my now-sopping-wet shirt. I was dizzy as hell.

Angry and shaking, I went back to the neck and yanked on the hook. Half of its trachea came out. Another yank, the treble hook came out, and the son of a bitch really began to bleed. My mind drifted suddenly to the mysterious box of Kotex in my mother's closet. I let the turtle hang, put my equipment together, tied myself back up, and watched for the dust trail announcing my mother's return.

She came, untied me, and saw the hanging turtle. "So, you got one?"

"Yep, I'm going to take it to Drag."

"You can't put it in the trunk because I have books in there."

So I dragged the son of a bitch up the bank with the rope connected to the one claw and put it on the backseat floorboard. I was so weak that I fell into the passenger seat.

I was thirsty and hungry; my bloody hands were still shaking, and I was about to throw up. The twenty-minute ride home seemed endless because the headless turtle kept scratching around the backseat floorboard. Worse was the smell inside our car, even with the windows open.

The combination of a rotten river creature that lived in mud, its dried blood on my skin and clothes, and the odor of fear from a ten-year old boy was too much for my mother to take. "Don't come in the house without hosing off outside somewhere. Leave your clothes outside and I'll burn them in the trash barrel."

I stumbled out of the car and promptly threw up my pickle loaf sandwich and Kool-Aid on my clothes and in the ditch beside Drag's house. Then I dragged the turtle across the walk and to his back porch door. He heard the commotion, came out, and said,

"Damn, that's a big one. All by yourself? From the pump station? How long has it been dead?"

"Three hours."

"You are a mess. Does your mother know about this? I should clean it now. Wanna help?"

"Okay, I guess, but I'm going home and take a bath first."

Truth was, I didn't want to help. I had spent too much time with that son of a bitch already. News of a boy catching and killing a snapping turtle traveled fast, and watching Drag clean one was a big event. By the time I walked down to his backyard, Herm and the Sturgeon brothers were there, wanting to know every detail. I told them but left out the parts about my never knowing what I was doing and how scared I was through the whole ordeal. They could not believe that the three claw marks on my neck had come from the turtle.

Around sundown Drag had removed tissue that hid the tenderloins under the shell and proudly showed them to us. He took them inside, fried both, and brought them outside for the boys to eat. It was chewy and, well, I just couldn't get the images of that bastard looking at me as it came out of the water, or my last yank at his trachea.

Drag cooked turtle soup all through the night and brought some down to us the next afternoon. I was upstairs, and I heard him scold my mother about me being too young to catch snapping turtles.

"He needs to learn how to take care of himself," I heard her say. "The sooner the better. As long as he doesn't drown or lose a finger, I'm okay with it. He had blood all over his shoes and clothes and somehow got clawed on his neck. So far, so good."

Drag left me a twenty-dollar bill, which must have impressed my mother, because that week she made me a new shirt for school. Among her many talents, she was an experienced seamstress, and from time to time would have me pick out the material at Penny's in Jacksonville for her to sew. I had picked those three yards last summer, so her sewing it this summer was a sign that I was on her good side, at least for the moment.

My reputation around town grew immediately—even the old ladies wanted to feel the turtle claw scabs. And, of course, I began to embellish the ordeal, always leaving out the part where I was scared shitless the whole time.

I had been wanting to buy a rod and reel for a long time and had been looking at the black-and-white Zebco in the Gamble store window all summer. It cost half my turtle earnings; I bought it the next day. Added to my two-pole arsenal, I could now cast farther east from the concrete platform and catch the big ones.

I settled in to arriving, stepping out of jail, moving my operation to the pump station platform, and putting my stringer behind the grate. The Dodgers were having a great season behind the pitching of Don Newcomb and the hitting of Jackie, and I was catching so many keepers my mother would give them away to her friends.

With the summer winding down, I had explored every inch of the pump station's world. I was never bored. I tried my luck fishing from the bank of the Illinois River without success. The current was too strong, and I had no idea where the fish were. I gave up on it quickly but liked to go watch the barges filled with grain as they went up and down the river. I would wave at the guys on the boats, and they would wave back. I would always think they were living exotic lives, probably headed to New Orleans, wherever that was.

I became more drawn to the big snake and its daily movements. Its habit would be to move from the east bank across the channel to the west and do what . . . I wasn't sure. But it always moved around the same time every day, so I would set myself and watch it. After that first day, I began to think of it as just another animal in our pump station zoo.

I had decided it was a diamondback water snake from pictures I'd found in our *Lincoln Library*. It was at least five feet long, almost my height.

I had gotten good at using my Zebco and thought maybe I could catch the snake. I couldn't catch it like a fish but snag it with a bass plug like Herm Kund used when he fished for bass at Vortman's pond. He let me borrow a green Lazy Ike plug with two treble hooks on it.

The next afternoon I put the plug on my leader and watched. My plan was to wait until it was on the water, cast and snag him, and bring him to shore. And then what?

On time, the snake entered the water. I cast a couple of times and missed. The next one landed on its back but didn't snag. Next, I cast the plug on the other side of its body and dragged it across. It caught, and the same idiot who had panicked earlier in the summer now had an angry snake longer than he was tall on his rod. But this time it was worse. Much worse.

I backed up away from the bank and into the area toward the station. The reel string and the snake came along. It was one angry, twisting, and writhing snake. It was strong, all five feet of it, as I fought to hold my grip. Just then, I saw mom's car dust coming.

I was on the wrong side of the station. I dropped my Zebco, jumped on the platform, picked up my tackle box, and retied myself.

I was sweating and I must have looked like hell, because my mother asked, "Are you okay? Your face is so red, you look sick."

I put my head down and walked up the bank. We turned around slowly, and I asked my mom to stop. I looked out over to the other bank. I could see the snake and the rod jumping up and down. It was using its body like a rope on the ground when you snap one end and make it dance through the other end.

I adjusted the wing window and continued to look as we drove away. A dark cloud hovered over me in the car. What was I going to do with it? It wasn't food. Drag wasn't going to buy it. It had been my friendly companion all summer. We'd had our own cageless zoo with all the rest of the animals and me. I did this to it. I was ashamed like never before in my life.

I wasn't hungry at supper and went to bed early. A nightmare that still visits me years later began.

I'm tied to the tree on my bank, an anaconda crosses the ditch slowly, looking at me and flicking its tongue. I try to untie myself, but I can't. The snake begins to wrap itself around me. It is bigger than me and asks softly, "Why, what did I do to you?" It begins to squeeze. I can't move because it is heavier than me. Herm's Lazy Ike digs into my skin. I start to bleed. I can't breathe, and I wake up sweating and catching my breath.

I did not sleep the rest of the night. We returned to the station at the normal time the next morning, and I was so mad at myself that I didn't check the Dodgers' score. I watched the cloud of dust disappear and walked slowly over to the other side.

What I saw made me sick to my stomach. There were pieces of snakeskin and skeleton scattered around the area. The Lazy Ike was still hooked to a section of skin and bone. My Zebco was broken in three pieces. I sat down on the grass and imagined what had happened, the racoon mother probably in the middle of it all.

I had wanted my freedom the very first day, then took away the snake's. For no good reason. I mean, I enjoyed seeing that snake every day. Let me tell you, I still feel the shame of that day, seventy years later. And from time to time, still have that nightmare to remind me. In each dream the Lazy Ike is hooked into a different part of my body and the snake keeps asking, "Why?"

I did not fish that day. Instead, I retrieved Herm's plug and my broken rod and put them on the platform. Then I grabbed my lunch and climbed over the levee. I sat on the bank of the river the rest of the day and watched the barges go by.

Using the river water as a mirror, I was ashamed of whom I saw. Oh, sure, my three claw scars were noticeable markers that made me bigger on the outside. The old ladies were still wanting to touch it. But the scar on the inside was mine for life. No one could touch or see that one except me. Why had I taken the snake's freedom? I made a vow to never be so stupid again. My recurring dream made me the son of a bitch every time.

I untied the rope from the tree and both knots at the ends. I coiled it up and put it in the middle of the road. I added my tackle box, poles, and broken Zebco. Then I walked down the hill to the pump house, sat, and waited for my mother with my back to the wall. I scooted to the south so when she drove up, she could easily see me.

When she arrived, I climbed slowly up the hill, making sure she saw I was in no hurry. I wanted her to understand that I was done pretending to be tied up anymore.

"What happened to your rod?"

"I broke it. Just so you know, I've been untying myself all summer."

"At least you didn't drown. Get in, let's go." She was that kind of woman.

My Friend Chester Long

On Halloween Day 1997, Chester Long's light was flicked out by a westbound Baltimore and Ohio Railroad locomotive. He had been straddling his bike on the southwest side of the tracks, listening to the radio on his Walkman, which I had given him, and waiting for the freight train to roll through Bluffs as he had hundreds of times. Chester was fifty-five years old.

In that speck of time between being hit and killed instantly, Chester probably knew what hit him but didn't know that four days later, in his favorite jeans and red flannel shirt, he'd be smiling up at his goodbye friends as they told him how good he looked.

I met Chester Long in September 1950 at Bluffs Elementary School—it was my first and only time in first grade and Chester's second time of three. Decades later, this classmate of mine, who was often the object of cruel jokes when we were young, would give my family a permanent gift, one that always brings a smile to our faces even during a debate.

Though Mrs. Grimes had held him back again that year, she passed him to the next class the following year. Then, in 1954, Chester was sent home with a note from Principal Hatfield that ended his student days at that academic citadel.

"I didn't much care for Mrs. Hatfield to begin with," said

RAIL
CROSSING
ROAD

Chester's mother, Nellie Long. "After that note, I never said no other words to her again."

The Longs were tenant farmers just scratching out a living for the Westermeyer brothers on the bottom land just south of our town. They had five kids, Chester being number four.

Chester was legally blind; his state-issued glass lenses looked like Coke bottles. Also hard of hearing, his ears were constantly draining, sometimes down to his shirt collar, which was the reason the principal sent him home that day in 1954.

From the beginning, my mother, also a schoolteacher, worried about the Longs. "Hell, if Chester could see and hear, he'd probably read better than you," she'd tell me.

In this way, she introduced me to the concept of random fortune—me drawing the luckier card, as I slept in my own bed in town while Chester slept in a bed-less, dirt-floor room with two older brothers. I can still feel my fear the day I'd peeked into that dark, dank room and wondered how anyone could fall asleep there.

I left home for good in 1962. When I visited periodically, I would always find Chester to say hello, bring him a small gift, and pay homage to his hands. They reminded me of the old-time baseball glove that Babe Ruth wore in the 1940s—short and thick. Extra-large winter gloves were long enough for Chester's hands but too narrow for his fingers. Consequently, his hands were permanently winterized, red and chapped to medium-grade sandpaper. Delicate they were not. Strong, earthen, and often stained black in the fall from shucking walnuts from their hulls—Chester's hands symbolized the harsh lives of the tenant families I lived alongside daily.

I still remember how unimpressed I was when, in 1984, I shook basketball star Julius Erving's famous hands in a New York City hotel elevator. "Sorry, Julius," I said to myself, "your hands are minor league compared to Chester Long's, my God of hands."

None of the citizens who donated money for Chester's funeral and tombstone could tell you when, but at some point, his gentle presence had become an important thread in the fabric of everyday life in Bluffs.

When Nellie's husband died in 1981, she left the farmhouse and moved into town with Chester. The other four children had already moved away, so there were just the two of them living in a small house with linoleum floors. Nellie did laundry and ironed clothes to make ends meet, and Chester started making friends. He did seasonal manual work for shorthanded farmers and performed odd jobs like mowing grass for widows and delivering all the newspapers in town. Chester never went hungry and always had small bills from tips in his pocket, which he did not report to the IRS.

Chester was also best friends with the forty to fifty dogs who roamed around town. Dogs in those times ran loose. No one "walked" or "leashed" their dogs, and, for sure, no one had a plastic bag. If you had an "indoor" dog, all you did was let it outside to do its business and socialize with the other dogs. The town was like a dog park with Chester right in the middle. He knew each of their names, and they loved him for petting them with those amazing hands.

Shyness, courteousness, and reliability were Chester's strong suits, not elaborate conversation. Mostly you asked him questions to which you knew the answers and to which he would respond, "Yeup," in two syllables. Sometime in the mid-1980s, before Chester's death, my daughter and I were debating, probably not in Bluffs, but maybe, and one of us kept answering, "Ye-up." The other said, "Like Chester Long would say, Ye-up!"

And that was the beginning of it. We'd adopted this up-periscope response to alert the other person to proceed with caution. Since then, this "two-syllable" word has evolved within our circles into an effective baloney detector that can be expressed in several degrees: A one-second "Ye-up" puts you, the speaker, on notice. A two-second "Ye-up" puts your words under heavy suspicion. And a three-second "Ye-up" means there's bullshit spewing from your mouth, and everyone is laughing at you.

As in all families, we have differing opinions about many things. Chester's gift is a hedge against anyone drinking her own bathwater. It is a soft way of saying "no" with a "Ye-up."

Although his life is done, Chester's light continues to shine brightly in our lives.

Punk

Everyone knows *who* turned Orville Morthole's outhouse into a roman candle and burned it down on a crisp November night in 1960. It was a spectacular event that made four boys legends overnight.

The great mystery is *how* they did it.

Curly Batterfield, our part-time constable, investigated the arson case but it fizzled because everyone in town knew *why*. Truth be told, he was relieved they hadn't burned Orville's house down, which would have forced the lawman to make some arrests. Instead, he never even brought the four suspects in for questioning, and they remain at-large. Happily, I might add.

The event didn't end up in history books like the Great Fire of London or the Great Chicago Fire. But in our small village, anecdotal stories and opinions about that night have lit the town up for decades and turned the legends into mythical figures.

Now that Orville has died and is residing in hell, I can set the record straight. None of the guesses colored me as a suspect. I was a sophomore that year, and not a member of the school's prestigious Brain Crew. But by chance, I was in the middle of the beginning and the secret at the end of the great event.

The four legends, still living, have given me permission to tell the rest of the story.

Four years after that epic night, Dirty Dave, one of the suspects, and I crossed paths at home during mutual breaks from college. We were laughing about the *reported* smile on our volunteer fire chief's face the moment the first explosion sent the burning roof straight up in the air.

I use *reported* because three of the prime suspects were on the football field at the time playing for the home team and were therefore unable to witness Chief Luther's reaction. The players did, however, call time-out to watch when the burning roof lit up the sky.

The referees enjoyed the show so much one of them gave the touchdown signal and allowed the time-out to extend till the end.

Lore got the roof up to one thousand feet at times, but Ralph, the fourth suspect, who by the age of eighty had successfully registered twelve patents with the US government, said it was "about one hundred feet."

Among other things that day, Ralph had run the numbers. Our Great Fire's mastermind, he was moving the down-marker with the chain gang when the roof lifted off. Everyone in the bleachers saw him.

The citizens said that our fire chief nodded his head in approval as they all watched the flaming shithouse roof wobble down to earth. And most eyewitnesses, all in the stands at the edge of town, swore the burning roof drifted slowly downward as if it had a parachute attached to it.

Yet, in front of the crowd, our esteemed fire chief did not hurry.

Instead, he got out of his bleacher seat and walked down the sideline to his car with his head up watching the sky light up in intermittent bursts of color. Everyone said he was smiling.

He drove his 1956 black Hudson slowly to the fire station where he met three other volunteers. Since there were only one hundred forty-seven houses and sixteen functioning out-houses in the village, they knew exactly where and what was burning.

The firemen turned north on Route 100, rolled over the Wabash railroad tracks, turned east on Main Street, and then five streets up to Oakes Street to our Great Fire. The trip took less than five minutes, and they never turned the siren on.

Upon arrival, the volunteers watched the fireworks to make sure they didn't burn any houses down. They didn't lift a finger to put it out. Orville, the town's ogre, who never went to the football games, was there screaming at the volunteers to turn their big hose on and save his shithouse.

Howard Six did turn the truck's hose on but sprayed Orville back into his shitty little house instead. The firemen and townspeople, who had driven there directly from the game, laughed and enjoyed the show.

Even Mayor Knoepal, a man of few words, was heard to comment, "It's probably Orville's first shower."

They let the structure burn to the ground while the shit and piss burned like lava from a volcano. There was a whiff of gasoline in the smoke and the stench drove people back away from the pit that Herm had walked into seven days before.

THE FOUR LEGENDS:
Herm, Dirty, Henny, and Ralph

Seniors that year, the four boys worked together doing sea-sonal, summer farm jobs all through high school. Jobs like castrating piglets, bucking bales, cutting weeds out of beans, and detasseling corn on stilts paid good wages to use their young bodies. The money they earned went into their family's coffers because all of them were poor.

Resting on a fence in eighty-degree weather, looking at the heavy mud on their stilts' bottoms, bleeding from the corn leaf cuts on their necks and faces, desperately drinking water, and telling stories before they got up and clomped down another row of six-foot corn forged lifelong bonds between them.

The four had winter jobs also. Dirty worked at his father's IGA store on Main Street. Herm, who always had a red shop rag hanging out of back pocket, pumped gas and changed oil at Hap Vortman's Texaco station.

Henny lived out of town on Highway 100 and worked on his family's farm raising pigs and driving a tractor. As a freshman, Ralph started keeping books for Henny's uncle who was running a hog breeding company up on the bluffs of Oxville behind Henny's house.

To them, going back to school in September was the start of *their nine-month vacation.* No more holding a squealing pig while another slit his ball sac and cut his testicles out followed by a douse of kerosene to keep the flies away from the bleeding wound. Or no more bucking hay bales into a barn with a bull snake wriggling out the side looking straight at you.

Nope, school was a breeze and getting good grades to these four was as easy as downing a double dip, chocolate ripple ice cream cone from Lecie's Drug Store.

It was a rural high school whose enrollment was always around one hundred students. The football coach named them the *Brain Crew* because they chose to eat sack lunches together upstairs in the study hall instead of with the rest of the students downstairs at the cafeteria. "They have more brains than food," he had said when he christened them their freshman year.

Their collective was a unique phenomenon of that place and time. One of the boys' homes didn't have running water. Two had outhouses, Ralph's being a custom two-and-a-half holer (one for the smaller children). Only Dirty's family had central heating.

Herm and his deaf father did have a toilet, but they had to break the stool water in the winter mornings. Herm would later become a leader in California deaf education and at the threshold of cochlear implant transition teaching.

The two poorest boys, Herm and Ralph, never got up from lunch hungry. Dirty and Henny, who had more access to food, always shared. By their senior year, they could have come up with a dollar between them for four hot lunches, but they knew their study hall tradition was more stimulating than anything that happened in their classes.

Their teachers—not exactly the cream of the crop ended up at rural schools—knew the Brain Crew was way ahead of their curves and often asked them for help when they, the teachers, were confused.

It would often happen at the blackboard; the teacher would turn back to one of the members sitting in class and ask for help or affirmation of a point. The boy would oblige grace-fully, and the lesson would continue. They were never cocky or loud. Only at lunch would they share the details and gossip about the teachers' shortcomings among themselves.

Of course, the teachers and students talked about the influence the boys had on classes, which meant that everyone in town knew. So when one of their own was tricked into walking into Orville's shit pit on a cool October night, everyone in town tapped their fingers on the table, raised their eyes, and waited to see what the geniuses would do.

Orville Morthole was the town ogre. Henny named him the *troll* from *The Three Billy Goats Gruff.* There are many fantastic illustrations of the troll, so close your eyes and imagine. That year, Orville might have been sixty-something years old. He lived alone.

His house was in the village, but no one considered him a citizen. He never went to church or any school functions, or bought food in the village. He never even went to the Legion's annual burgoo celebration, which attracted hundreds of people from surrounding communities. He always left town on Friday afternoon and returned late. Dirty always said Orville visited a whore in Springfield. Of the four, Dirty was into those kinds of things.

Rumor had it Orville got his money in the mail from the government for being nuts.

He had a mangy, three-legged mongrel he kept tied to a chain outside. He would throw scraps to it for food, including chicken bones. A group of humane society–type women knocked on his door one time and asked him to take better care of the dog. He told them, "Mind your own fucking business." The whole town felt sorry for the dog.

He would drive over the sidewalk and park his car in his yard and never cut his grass. He would shoot dogs walking around his property with a pump BB gun. He never gave any candy to kids on trick-or-treat night, so all the kids knew not to go.

His outhouse had been tipped over fourteen consecutive years on Halloween as the consequential *trick*.

His face was covered with blackheads. So much so that the mothers urged their children to wash their faces nightly or they would "start looking like Orville Morthole."

His most insidious trait was how he was always squishing his lips like a dying carp gasping for breath on the bank. It was so repulsive that people in conversation would make an "Orville" with their mouth when they referenced something or someone they hated.

HERM

I lived across the alley from Herm, and he always let me tag along like I was his younger brother. We had spent thousands of sweet hours playing in that alley growing up and he continued to include me even when he was a high school senior and me a lowly sophomore. I idolized my older *brother*.

On that fateful October night, we were headed to Dirty's house to listen to the hot new single "Stuck on You" by the Drifters. His family had the only stereo in town that could play a 45 record, and it was where we went to listen to all the new songs.

We didn't make it.

Like all the village's teenage boys, we had Halloween mischief on our minds. We didn't have any eggs in our pockets to throw on car windshields so they would freeze, so the default meant tipping over the outhouses along the path to Dirty's house. As a rule, we never tipped over the outhouses of people we liked.

We walked the familiar path that cut through the various yards and knew the troll's was on our way. We were excited to be the first to push his shithouse over that Halloween.

We could see the outline of Orville's outhouse. The path was in front of it, and Herm and I were walking side-by-side when Herm walked straight into the pit full of shit and piss.

I've corrected many people over the years. "He didn't fall in, he walked in!"

The troll had moved his outhouse back just enough that we didn't see the trap he had set.

I remember most the stinking belches that came from Herm sinking into hell with his shoes on. *Blwap, blwaap, blwaaap* as the pit farted upwards, caused by Herm's sudden entrance into the noxious bog. He hit the bottom and was neck-deep in Orville's shit.

A personal note here: Our familiar network of paths through town were worn bare one person wide. When there were two people headed to the same place, sometimes they walked single file, sometime tandem, meaning one person was walking along the path, not on it. That night, Herm and I were talking, walking in tandem, and he was the unlucky one. It could have easily been me, but I was on the other side. To this day, he greets me with "Hello you lucky bastard." We both laugh. I was.

Herm was moaning, "I'm going to die, I'm going to die" in a voice I didn't know. Then "help me, come on help me." I could see then he was neck-deep in shit as he plunged toward the side nearest me. He put his hands on the top of the path but couldn't get any purchase with either hand or foot to lift himself out.

I squatted in front of him, held out both arms, and got hands full of shit. And when he pulled, I almost flew into the bog. I let go, he fell backward, ears under but face up.

It was an awful moment highlighted by the smell of Orville's aged shiss.

Desperate to help, I lay on my belly and snaked up to the edge and held both hands out to him. God, it stunk. This time, however, I was able to hold my purchase with my knees dug into the ground, and Herm pulled his body over the edge and crawled out. He was in shock, shaking and moaning. I didn't know what the fight-or-flight reflex was at the time, but I knew he was hurting badly.

In charge now, only because I was the more coherent one at that moment, I told Herm to follow me. We got off the path and headed to the back of my house where I knew there was a garden hose. It was a cold night, the water was icy as well, but I sprayed his hands, head, ears, and face. He whimpered and began to cry. My big *brother*.

He sat on the sidewalk at the back of our house and began to take his clothes off. I ran inside and got two big wool blankets. My mother came out of the house then. She considered Herm her son also, and pulled his shoes off. We then hosed him completely and he began to shiver and then vomited. The outside temperature was 40 degrees. I felt so sorry for him.

We wrapped him in the blankets, and I took him upstairs to our bathtub. We didn't have a shower. My mother threw in bubble bath, dish detergent, and bleach, and we let him clean himself.

I found a sweatshirt that came close to fitting him. I wrapped him again in the blankets and put him in my bed. I lay on a smaller couch and in about an hour, I heard him say, "I'm going to kill the son of bitch."

I went downstairs and shoveled all his clothes out into the back alley. Then I walked to Orville's outhouse and tipped it over toward the open shit pit. I wanted to shove it into the bog, but I wasn't strong enough to do it. Neither of us slept that night.

I went into Herm's house early in the morning, his father was deaf and still sleeping, and found some clothes and shoes for him. I dropped those off and went to Lecie's Drug Store and bought Herm a toothbrush and toothpaste.

He was dressed when I returned home and sitting at our kitchen table, staring down at some eggs and bacon my mother had made. Normally ravenous teenage eaters, we ate nothing that morning.

Luckily, we had a football game that Friday night and a player had to attend school that day to be able to play that night. We walked to school and on the way, he repeated, "I'm going to kill the son of bitch."

In a moment of sixteen-year-old clarity, I said, "Wait until after the football game; we won't win if you don't play."

It had been a traumatic night for both of us. I ended up with some of Orville's shit on my shirt and pants, so they went to the pile to be burned in the alley with Herm's clothes. I kept replaying the events over and over, especially when Herm almost pulled me in. In those horrible moments, I would have done anything to save him, including jumping into the shithole myself.

Finally, it was lunchtime, and I went to the cafeteria downstairs like always. I was still out of it, but I was hungry and ate cautiously to avoid throwing up. As I was finishing, Herm tapped me on the shoulder and said, "Come upstairs with me."

The Brain Crew was waiting for us. I sat down and they began to interrogate me with Herm intermittingly chiming in saying "See, I told you so."

Yes, it was a hard-to-believe story. Occasionally, one of them would utter "no shit?" or "that's a crock of shit!" or "you were neck-deep in shit?" or "you are full of shit!" Sure, they were on the edge of their seats, laughing at both of us.

Neither Herm nor I laughed. Quickly, the other three calmed down and began to discuss a response they would be proud of.

Ralph and Henny promptly vetoed the idea of killing Orville. Of the three, Dirty would have provided the rifle and bullets and watched. But the two who lived "in the country" were more levelheaded and forward-thinking.

Dirty came around quickly and told Herm, "I don't want to be visiting you in the Joliet State Penitentiary for the rest of my life." They continued to have big fun.

Ralph, besides having an IQ of 180, had a photographic memory. He mentioned a phrase he had read in some Italian literature that went something like *revenge is a dish served better cold*. The other students were jealously wondering why I was enjoying an audience with the esteemed Crew—they were famous for not letting other lowly students enter their physical kingdom.

But there I was, and as they plotted an appropriate response, they chose me to hide their fingerprints at the crime scene. It remains the greatest honor of my life.

But how?

After school and before that night's football game started, Ralph walked to the path that went by Orville's outhouse and did quick measurements to determine its volume.

Seeing Ralph walk in town or on the highway toward his home was nothing out of the ordinary. Head up and eyes forward, his gait was maybe a step slow; he was never an athlete.

He never raised his voice or showed any outward emotion. He awed his classmates in his quiet way. They anointed him president each year—no need to hold a vote with him in your midst. His vice president each year by default, Sue Bridgman, always described Ralph as being "cool as a cucumber," which around those parts was the ultimate compliment.

Orville's car was gone, probably to see that whore in Springfield. Ralph went inside the outhouse quickly to check how secure the roof was and to guess how much it weighed.

Ralph then walked to Rosie's tavern on Main Street, ordered a hamburger, fries, and a Coke and drew up his plan on a Budweiser paper napkin. Ralph would graduate from the University of Illinois two years later with an electrical engineering degree and we all agreed that his plan to blow up Orville's shithouse was the beginning of his patenting career, one in which he blew apart one-hundred-pound chain links with C-4.

Acoustical mooring release system
Patent number: 4616590, Ralph E. Clements

In that night's game, Herm had the Bluejay uniform on, but his mind was still on the smell he couldn't get off his skin. He never caught a pass.

Thankfully, our levelheaded quarterback, Henny, threw two touchdown passes to Dirty to win our next-to-the-last game. Henny would later get his MS in agriculture engineering and be an early advocate for no-till farming.

Ralph ran the first-down marker for the chain gang, but his mind was on fireworks and an article he had recently read about C-4, a new plastic explosive.

What I remember most that night was how Dirty, Henny, and Ralph put their arms around Herm after the game, led him to Henny's 1949 Ford, and drove out of town to the junction for cheeseburgers.

I watched the taillights head out of town and knew they wouldn't be talking about loving one another and all the sappy stuff. Unlike the artificial "team bonding" programs of the twenty-first century, their bond was formed by sweat, blood, blisters, and work fatigue that welded their lives together permanently.

Henny brought Dirty back to town, dropped Ralph off at his country house, and took Herm to Likes' farmhouse for the rest of the week. The four had decided it was best to keep Herm there to insure he wouldn't murder Orville.

Because I was recruited to be an accomplice by the Crew, I know the details of how the caper was planned and executed. Henny picked me up on the Sunday afternoon, we drove to Winstead's in Jacksonville, and we set the plan for our next Friday night football game.

But first, continuing their levity, the crew was interested in Ralph's reconnaissance of Orville's outhouse, specifically what Orville used to wipe his ass. They were disappointed he didn't report *corncob*.

Instead, Orville was using an old Montgomery Ward catalogue, which was a notch above a corncob. Third in the village's ass-wipe hierarchy came pages from a Sears and Roebuck catalogue. I never understood why one catalogue's page was rated socially higher than the other, and then there was toilet paper at the top.

The crew listened to Ralph's plan: Naturally he was the mastermind, but Herm was to light the fuse, a collective requirement by the Crew. All of us would have to be seen at the football game when the shithouse blew.

Here's how it went down.

SUNDAY

I was chosen to go get the fireworks in Hannibal, sixty miles from our village, in my '54 Chevrolet that my grandmother had willed to me two years before. No one would pay attention to my absence or link it to what was going to happen.

I got the list from Ralph that Sunday afternoon. He had called the Fireworks Warehouse from Henny's family's phone that Saturday and decided what he needed and what it would cost.

He gave me an Illinois road map and marked the roads I would take to get to Hannibal, a drive of ninety minutes. I was to skip school Monday and get to the warehouse by 11 a.m.

The Crew gave me one hundred dollars to buy the following:

Four aerial shell cannons

Four twenty-five shot cakes, gold, green, blue, and red

Fifty feet of cannon fuse

Two three hundred shot Saturn missile rounds

Two packages of punk (compressed sawdust on a stick) to light the fuses in sequence

MONDAY

My mission was known only to the Crew, and I admit I imagined myself as Jessie James, especially on my return with the fireworks in the back of my trunk. The Likes' farm was on my way home, so I unloaded them in their big barn and covered them with gunny sacks as instructed.

I drove straight to school and told the principal I was feeling better. That was Monday.

TUESDAY

Henny, Herm, and Dirty had football practice after school, so I was assigned to take Ralph to the barn. He checked the fireworks and in his own soft words said, "Great job." I still remember how proud I was.

In my presence, he drew a rectangle on the dirt floor, always referring to his Budweiser napkin. He then moved the fireworks into the rectangle, sat down and looked at the stack, and shook his head.

"We're going to have to build a model here," he told me, "because I want to be exactly sure where to place each explosive."

Ralph told me to see Dirty after football practice and get as much cardboard as possible from the back of his family's IGA store.

WEDNESDAY

I picked up the cardboard from the back of Dirty's IGA store after school and Ralph and I drove straight to the barn. He had *borrowed* a stapler from the math teacher's desk and a roll of duct tape from the school janitor's room.

The three other Brain Crew members were at football practice and behaving normally.

With Ralph's direction, we stapled together a replica 4' x 5' and 8' high. He then stapled the seat exactly four feet from the ground across our model. Next, he taped an A-frame roof together and placed it on the top like a hat.

He then announced, "I have to go back and take another look at how I'm going to arrange the fuses."

THURSDAY NIGHT

After dark, Dirty and Ralph walked on the familiar path to the troll's outhouse, and with Dirty holding a penlight, Ralph squatted low and looked closely at the back of it. In five minutes, Ralph said, "Okay, I got it, let's go." It was Ralph's photographic memory at its best.

The two returned to the barn and there the plan was set in motion.

FRIDAY MORNING

Ralph would skip school the next morning to tie the fuses in the right order. He said he needed daylight to do his work. The remaining three would go to school just like normal.

I, Jessie James, would drive out to the barn at noon to pick up Ralph and the fireworks. We both went to school that afternoon with the explosives in my car.

Ralph had supper at Rosie's Tavern, and I drove by and picked him up at 5:30 p.m.

6 PM

The football game was to start at seven and Orville usually left town by five.

We parked two blocks from the shithouse and each of us took a roundabout way to our target. I carried the fireworks in a gunny sack and Ralph carried his fuses and the punk.

Ralph arranged the following sequence.

First, he placed the four aerial cannons along the seat to blow off the roof. He duct-taped them to the seat and tied their fuses together so they would explode upward simultaneously.

Second, he placed the four twenty-five-shot cakes in the four corners of the seat and fused them so they would blow in two-minute intervals after the roof had been blown off.

Third, he set the two three-hundred-shot Saturn missile rounds on the floor on each side, facing each other, so the explosions would light the sidewalls.

Lastly, he threaded the three different fuses through holes in the back and then tied different lengths of punk to them. It was six twenty by that time, so we needed to hurry back to the football field.

But he wasn't done. He got on my shoulders—he only weighed 150 pounds, of which 50 was his brain—and tacked a nylon parachute's two corners on each side of the A-frame. He said quietly, "I'm not sure it will get high enough, but what the hell."

As agreed, we then went to the back of the locker room where it opened to the outdoors and Herm was given the honor of lighting three sticks of punk.

Dirty arrived late and admitted he had "pissed a bit of gasoline in the shithole." He was like that, always working outside the lines, including the year before when he bought a seat belt for his dad's '58 Ford.

Typical of the Crew's intelligence, seat belts would start to become mandatory eight years later, but there Dirty was, wearing a seat belt like Roger Ward, racing around town like he was at the Indy 500.

Ralph stayed. I had to hold the three sticks of smoking punk in my teeth because I needed both hands to drive my stick shift Chevy to Orville's street.

It was dark. My heart was up in my throat as I kneeled to light the first one, waited for one minute, lit the second, waited another one minute, and lit the third. Ralph had cal-culated the fuse/punk lag time to be just over an hour.

I got back in my car and returned to the game. The roof blew at eight-ten, just as the third quarter had begun. Ralph looked up from his watch, made eye contact with me down the sideline, and winked.

The rest is history.

Separation of Church and Sex

She turned off the car lights and then the engine, turned to him, unbuttoned her white blouse, reached around, and unsnapped her brassiere. It wasn't pitch-black where she parked, but close, so she took his right hand as if he were blind and put it on her right breast. She didn't say a word.

He was sixteen. She was thirty-five. It was the winter of 1950. It happened so fast he didn't have time to wonder if God was watching.

She pulled him close, kissed him, and whispered, "Go ahead and kiss my nipple." While he was kissing her right breast, she turned toward him more, took his left hand, and put it on her right breast.

When he kissed her left breast, she pulled him close to her body with both arms, tilted her head, and shook. He had no idea what had happened. He did, however, know what happened when she put her hand under his shirt and pinched his nipple hard.

She kissed him gently and said, "You've never done this before have you, Burl." It was a statement, not a question.

It was a freezing winter night, and even with their physical heat, which had steamed up the windshield, they were getting cold. She had estimated they might have twenty minutes before the risk of being seen would be too high. She calmly reattached her brassiere, buttoned her blouse, and put her hand on his leg.

"I know you are surprised. We can do this again if you want. Let me know. I'll drop you off."

"I'll walk back. Thanks, though."

Earlier, Ruth had offered him a ride home after the church's youth meeting. She'd drove past his house, crossed Route 100 to the other side of town, turned slowly into a familiar alley, and parked her car between two garages. The town's streets were blacktopped, but the alleys were a mixture of gravel, dirt, and cinders. She had driven slowly to minimize the alley's crackling sound and not draw attention to the car.

Ruth, a teller at the only bank in town, had carefully chosen that location. It was a small, rural village, and they both knew whose garages they were in between. On the left was Bill Olsen's; he was a widower who worked the second shift at the CIPS power plant, six miles away. The other had been vacant since Leah Comerford's death two months earlier, and her two children hadn't yet decided what to do with the property.

The village had three grocery stores, two gas stations, two barbers, and two bars—everyone knew everyone, including the dogs' names. Her biggest fear was that someone in town would see them. She knew if anyone got a whiff that she was alone with an admired teenage boy, she would be tarred, feathered, and run out of town. When she finally did turn into the alley with him in the car, her hands were noticeably shaking.

Besides being the youth group's Wednesday leader, Ruth was also the church's piano player, a leader at Thursday prayer meetings, and a fine Christian woman. Burl and his parents were members of the same Southern Baptist Church.

According to the teenage boys' committee that congregated in the village's twenty-four-hour laundromat every night, she was one of the five prettiest women in town. When she stepped out of her house, she always looked like a Hollywood actress. Her brightly colored clothes drew attention to her womanly figure, and the combination of her red lipstick and red hair drove the teenage boys' committee crazy.

She sang duets from the Baptist hymnal with her husband, Tom, who was the song leader during Sunday services. Burl always looked forward to their singing more than the boring morning sermon. Like all the boys, he fantasized about Ruth's body, but to actually kiss her breasts . . . he never believed that would happen in a million years.

Tom was the local plumber and famous logger in the county. He became a legend years before when he lifted two ten-pound carp out of the mud at the same time. Tom liked Burl and often invited him, the only teenager, to join his adult group of loggers in the Scott County drainage ditches. Burl admired Tom almost as much as he admired his own father.

Dazed, Burl took the long way home and came to when he walked by the still-open Rose's Tavern. He was never allowed in the place because the men were playing cards, drinking beer, and cussing—all terrible sins according to his parents. He tiptoed up the stairs in his house, skipping the two stairs that squeaked, so they wouldn't notice he had come in later than usual from church.

He lay in bed, eyes wide open, waiting to feel the Wabash coal train rumble through the village on its way to the power plant fifteen miles away. Their house was a football field from the tracks and shook more or less, depending on the number of loaded coal cars the train was pulling.

Soon he heard the familiar whistle and knew the outside wall of his upstairs room would shake. He normally used the shaking as the time to pray and go to sleep. Instead, he suddenly sat up and asked himself, *"Was she mad at me for walking home?"* As he'd been walking down the alley, she'd driven slowly by him and handed him his bible through the window. He had left it in her car. She hadn't said a word.

He rolled the night's tape backward. It was like she had hypnotized him and put him in a trance. She knew, but he didn't, that squeezing his tit would make him cum. It felt like the rifle shot would go through his jeans. Her kiss was softer than the ones he had experienced with the two "loose" girls in town. They were always trying to tempt him and had succeeded that past summer. He had felt guilty since and had prayed with his eyes open several times for God's forgiveness.

Feeling the goose bumps come up on Ruth's breasts when he touched her nipples had surprised him, then her mysterious reaction. What was that?

The youth meeting's topic that night had been about the Second Commandment. Ruth had brought a small Mayan statue as an example and told them that it was a sin to even think about false idols. Like the rest of the church leaders, she consistently pushed the church message that God monitored everyone's thoughts, good and bad. Good thoughts got you to heaven, bad, dirty ones sent you to burn in hell. Dancing was a sin.

Eyes still wide open, he thought about Ruth's amazing breasts. In his short prayer, he asked God for forgiveness if Ruth was mad at him for walking home.

He woke up early, recited, like a trained parrot, the mandatory Lord's Prayer with his parents at breakfast, and went to school. His first class was English, and as he looked around the room at the girls' breasts, he realized his frame of reference had suddenly changed. The image of Ruth's breasts popped up in his brain and stayed there; his classmates had suddenly become just girls. At that moment he realized he would have to pretend as if everything was normal in his life when it wasn't. He could privately relive his new experience and just keep his mouth shut.

After five years of celibacy, Ruth's body had won the battle over caution. She felt she had to do something to relight her fire inside before menopause arrived. After careful and painful consideration, Ruth had decided that Burl was the safest gamble to help her. She knew he was a virgin, a healthy teenage boy, and was a better bet to keep quiet than any other men she had considered.

It had all begun in August 1939 during her get-into-high-school physical with Dr. Joe Panella and his wife, Kay, a nurse. They practiced in the only doctor's office within a one-hundred-mile radius. Both were immigrants from the exotic island of Cuba. Paralyzed by polio years before, Dr. Joe practiced in a wheelchair.

Their office was in the front of the house they lived in; their door was always open. The two were famously kind and caring. Everyone knew them or knew about them. Over time Kay became Dr. Kay; they were the most revered people in the region.

High school physicals were a formality, and Kay was always in the room with the girls while the mothers sat in the waiting room. Dr. Joe and Kay knew the teenage girls would be more honest with them, especially during this more vulnerable time in their lives.

Ruth had gotten goose bumps during her pelvic exam and had a quick physical release in front of both.

Dr. Joe and Kay had looked at each other, eyes raised, and Dr. Joe said, "*Ella es una chica de sangre caliente.*"

Kay asked her if she knew what had happened.

"Not exactly," Ruth had said but then went on to tell them how she could make herself feel good at home alone in her bed. Then she asked, "What does *sangre caliente* mean?"

Kay told her that it was healthy, that not all girls were as quick as she was, and that God had given her a very special gift.

"Don't let anyone tell you differently" were Kay's parting words.

As she rode home, the fourteen-year-old smiled at the good news from Dr. Kay. She had impressed Ruth with words that would stay with her for life. There was not one person she could tell, not her mother, and for sure not her Sunday school teacher, who was always connecting the pleasure of one's body with sin. She vowed then, as the wind blew in from her wing window on the way home, that she would follow Dr. Kay's advice from that day forward.

Twenty-one years later, she was still attractive enough to get stares at the Jacksonville Kroger store, even though she was a bit heavy after her second child five years before. Her husband had not shown any interest since. She often asked God to restore Tom's interest, but so far, he hadn't delivered. She thought God was testing her faith.

She wasn't interested in getting a divorce. She loved and admired her husband as everyone else did in town. She was a well-known Christian woman who sang beautifully at special events all over the county, the mother of two children, and a popular teller in the village bank. She knew how much money everyone had in his checking account. Everyone knew her and the car she drove.

No one knew, however, how frustrated she had become in the private part of her life. Her faith challenged her in two ways. Was it a cross God wanted her to bear, or should she use the gift He had given her? She was paralyzed in that conflict until she found herself looking forward to a sixteen-year-old boy entering the bank. He would always wait, out of turn, to deposit with her, not the other teller.

His parents were members of her church, he was the star quarterback on the football team, an A student, decent looking, and had gumption, a word seldom used to describe a teenager in the village. She noticed him staring at her cleavage when she was writing his deposit receipt. He had not hidden his looking, and it felt good to her. Thus, over many deposits, she chose him to help her and maybe, help him too.

As she sat in her car behind the bank the next morning, she reviewed the night's events. He was calm and didn't reject me. *I knew my appetite hadn't changed and thank God my body still responds. Thank you, Dr. Kay.*

Of course, he was quick, he's sixteen. Hmm, I wonder if he was mad at me because he didn't let me drop him off at his house. Will he keep our secret? Will there be a next time?

Being an obedient son in a Christian home, Burl dutifully went to Sunday school and church, Thursday night prayer meeting, and the youth meetings. His parents never gave him a choice. Privately though, he didn't believe most of the bullshit they were always talking about. (He could never say the word "bullshit" out loud.)

He despised sitting in front of his Sunday school teacher. She had snow-topped mountains of pimples, dragon's breath, smelled like a cow, and was butt ugly. He would count the painful minutes as she lectured the class about not taking the Lord's name in vain or keeping the Sabbath holy, whatever that meant.

Her husband, the church's pastor, bagged groceries at the Kroger store twenty miles away. Burl had always thought that was an odd job for a person telling other people what to do. Burl considered his summer job of bucking bales a more important job, and it paid more.

But the grocery-bagger-preacher would pray on, often three times during his morning sermon. By the third, as Burl looked at the back of the congregation's heads, Burl knew he wasn't a true believer, especially if *that guy* had the key to heaven.

The prayer meetings? His geography teacher that year had shown pictures of voodoo seances, and he couldn't get those out of his mind while sitting in a pew listening to the various people pray to something, somewhere up in the sky.

From the beginning, he kept his eyes open because it felt too unnatural to close them in that strange setting. He had decided, over time, that it was just an opportunity for people to ask for special favors from God, like help heal Aunt Iris from her cancer or ask Fred Northcutt to come in and accept Christ as his savior. He had quit keeping score a while back, since it seemed God never healed anyone, and cancer always killed them.

He was, however, eager to go to church that next Sunday to see Ruth and confirm if what he thought had happened had really happened. Would she give him some signal? After the normal excruciating Sunday school hour, church started and Ruth and Tom sang the hymn "Nearer, Blessed Assurance, Jesus is Mine!"

"Blessed assurance, Jesus is mine! Oh, what a fore-taste of glory divine."

At the end, she took the song book from the music desk, rose, walked up the aisle, looked straight at him, and smiled. He took that as a yes.

Given their different daily trajectories and personal responsibilities, it was impossible for them to meet or talk without some church event excuse. Burl went to all the church activities, Ruth always smiled especially at him, and finally the next monthly youth meeting came. He arrived first, yes, he was eager, and stood on the church steps as she drove up on a rainy spring night.

She closed the door behind them, took his hand, and walked to the side of the sanctuary. She put his arms around her and hers around him and pushed her breasts against him.

"I'll give you a ride home tonight. I don't want you to get wet," she said with a wink.

That night's lesson was about not taking the Lord's name in vain and honoring your father and mother, the Third and Fifth Commandments. She used Burl as an example because everyone in town knew that he was a serious teenager who never cussed.

He heard her words but could only think about what might happen afterward. That night, she drove down the same dark alley, unbuttoned her blouse, and turned her back to him.

She said softly, "You should know how to unsnap a woman's brassiere, so go ahead, then lift it off my breasts."

The sixteen-year-old star quarterback fumbled awkwardly —his hands were shaking, and the whole process made Ruth laugh. Burl was terribly embarrassed; he hadn't fumbled the football the past two seasons.

Finally, she turned the dome light on and said, "There are two hooks, you must get both. See?"

See he did and, well, he knew what to do with what he saw. Her breasts free, the same results occurred for both.

Afterward, the dome light off, she asked him if he knew what he did for her. He didn't, of course, so she explained her climax response. (She assumed all women must have the same response, but she didn't know for sure, since discussions about personal sex were taboo in her world.) He did pay attention to her words as she compared how she felt to how it felt when he ejaculated. He was shocked at this new information and wondered why none of his older buddies had told him about this thing girls had.

With April came later sunsets and a smaller window to hide her Ford Fairlane after the youth meeting. Their brief times together had made Ruth feel alive again, and she so looked forward to stealing the time for herself. On their third meeting, Burl took the lead, unbuttoned her blouse, and smoothly unsnapped both hooks on her brassiere. Now literally feeling in familiar territory, he took his time and Ruth exploded bigger than normal. That her response made him feel important would be an understatement.

She then guided his hand under her skirt and between her

legs. (She had taken her panties off in the sanctuary's bathroom before the class.)

She said, "Feel me, carefully, be gentle." She took his hand and put it to his nose. "Smell what you do to me, taste me."

He did, and on the way home, and in geometry class the next day. He was one confused sixteen-year-old, not about the fifth axiom—the whole is greater than the parts—but did the syrup between her legs mean she was in heat like the female farm animals he knew about? Or something else? He decided before the class ended that he should understand her response, but he had no go-to person or book to ask.

Unless Ruth came up with a different plan for their secret rendezvous, that next time would have to wait until the fall, because the youth meetings had ended for the summer. He couldn't find anything in the school or town libraries; he had looked under sex but kept looking over his shoulder to make sure no one caught him. There were only pictures and prices of brassieres and panties in the Sears and Roebuck catalogue, a teenage boy's porn source at the time. He found no answer.

Burl was a sought-after worker in the hayfields because he was over six feet tall and strong. He made two cents a bale for picking it up in the field and throwing it in the barn. Some days he handled one thousand bales and made a whopping twenty dollars. This would be his second season working with seniors Bull Beddingfield and Stanley Likes. More than he had last summer, he looked forward to listening to their braggadocio about tits, asses, and legs and who was putting out with whom.

Unbeknownst to them, he had been touching a grown woman's breasts and more all winter. He listened for facts while they only talked in rumors and fantasies. According to them, they were getting laid every night. He bit his tongue.

At the end of May, during the crew's annual Top-of-the-Mountain Competition, a kind of who-is-the-strongest-man-of-all contest for the summer, Burl stacked thirteen bales high, and Bull and Stanley could only get twelve. Physical strength was most admired in the farm village, so Burl's having beaten the two older boys was big news that traveled fast. Ruth heard about it the next day in the bank, and it made her smile.

June brought Burl's first invitation from Tom to join his logging expedition, which included immediately cleaning the fish, and siding and scoring the filets as wives stood by to fry and make carp sandwiches. It was a welcome-to-summer party, and he didn't disappoint by contributing a twelve-pound carp to the feast. (Unlike Tom's fish, it took Burl two hands to lift the fish and put it in his gunny sack.)

Burl found himself standing in front of Ruth at the serving table. She handed him his sandwich and potato salad and asked mischievously, "You beat Bull and Stanley, now this fish. What happened to you this winter?"

He looked her straight into her eyes and said, "I've been studying the Ten Commandments and listening to you sing." Ruth blushed.

So, it was obvious the green light was on between them, but the summer light was preventing any rendezvous possibilities. Even without the meetings, Burl's life had become more complicated with the images of Ruth's amazing breasts appearing often in his brain.

Things changed at the end of June when Ruth was asked to take over the church's bookkeeping after Ina Korty had died.

The pastor had asked Ruth to accept God's calling, and she immediately started calculating how she could restart their secret sessions.

The church's basement consisted of three partitioned Sunday school rooms for the four-to-seven-year-old children. Each section had a low table and a few tiny chairs on one side and an adult chair for the teacher on the other side. The small, windowless business office was along the back wall next to the boys' bathroom.

At about the same time, the Wabash Railroad's depot manager gifted Burl with the part-time job as the locomotive roundhouse helper. It was the biggest and most important building in the county where the locomotives, which could only pull in one direction, went to get regular maintenance and turned around in the right direction.

As young boys, Burl and his buddies had spent many hours watching a huge engine roll slowly onto the turntable, turned by the operator, then moved inside the roundhouse for the next day's work. Sometimes, when the Lazy Susan's motor was out, the boys were asked to help push the lever and turn the huge engine manually. It was always great fun to test their strengths against a six-hundred-ton locomotive.

Burl's older neighbor had been the helper for two years but left to take a big-paying construction job in Chicago. Burl's was a "plum job" according to his mother. Everyone in town knew it was only offered to a responsible boy. Wabash never asked for applications.

Burl's duties were to fill the engines' oil cans, clean each cabin, wipe the brake surfaces, brush the firebox clean, and fill the sandbox. Like a horse groomer, his locomotives were in the stalls at night to be brushed and cleaned for the next day.

Wabash paid him two dollars an hour, and the amount of work depended on the locomotive traffic. It took him one week to learn all his duties but many weeks to relax in the poorly lit building filled with the magnificent machines and smelling like the combination of oil, ash, grease, and coal. After a week of training, the depot manager had given him the key to the door behind the building.

The July Fourth weekend went by, Burl turned seventeen, and Ruth played the piano while Tom sang his favorite solo, "The Old Rugged Cross":

"On a hill far away stood an old rugged cross, the emblem of suffering and shame."

On the way out of church, Ruth calmly isolated Burl and said, "I am doing the books here now on Wednesday nights. Come by at nine-thirty and we can talk more about the Ten Commandments."

On Wednesday night Burl walked down the dark street— the village did not have streetlights—and looked around carefully to make sure he saw no one. Her car was parked in front. He turned the knob on the usually locked church door. It was open and dark in the sanctuary. Ruth was standing there waiting, and he almost ran into her. She locked the door behind him, took his hand, and led him down the pitch-black stairs. When she turned the lights on, he realized they had complete privacy because there were no windows in the basement.

That they weren't alone in a dark, parked car made Burl shy and anxious. They were in a basement classroom for little kids.

She pointed him toward the bigger teacher's chair and then she sat on the lower table, facing him with her feet on the floor, their knees touching.

She kidded him about smelling like Lava soap and assumed he had come straight from the roundhouse.

She took his hands and put them to her nose and asked, "So you are still interested in learning more about the Commandments?"

Commandments had become the code word for their rendezvous. He nodded *yes* as he felt himself relaxing. It helped that she was holding his hands now in her lap.

"So, God gave me this body, and I am sure he wants you to understand how it works." She leaned toward him and said softly, "Unbutton my blouse so you can look at my breasts in the light."

He reached around her, unsnapped successfully, lifted her bra off, and kissed both breasts.

She leaned into and kissed him, noting that he was more aroused now than in the car.

Then she tilted back slowly and said, "Unbutton my skirt. It is on this side"—she pointed at the button—"then pull my panties off."

She put her ankles on his thighs to make it easier for him. Like the first time in her car, he was short of breath and his hands were shaking.

Staring at a mature woman's vagina, he waited for instructions. Because the kindergarteners' table was wider east to west, she scooted counterclockwise around so her head and feet were all on the table.

"Help yourself, look and touch my body, I want you to."

He soon got the answer about the syrup he'd felt from her vagina.

She sat up and touched his penis through his pants and said, "I don't have one of those, but I get excited just like you, and this is how I show it."

She had climaxed when he rubbed the inside of her legs.

She scooted back to sitting in front of him and instructed, "Now dress me. You need to know this too."

He fumbled a bit and they both laughed, which gave them a moment of levity both needed.

They walked upstairs, kissed, and she said, "Happy birthday, Burl," and winked at him. "Is next Wednesday, the same time, okay?" He nodded yes, then she said, "Next week will be your turn."

He slid out the door and walked the long way home.

A string of thoughts raced through his newly seventeen-year-old brain: *My turn? Do I know what she means? Kind of. What kind of commandment will that be?* At least he had gotten the answer to what the stuff was between Ruth's legs. For a naive moment, he thought he might be the only boy in the world who knew.

His week went by slowly. There were lots of in-and-out locomotives, and each night he worked his full four hours. Sunday came and Tom and Ruth sang "The Lily of the Valley."

"I have a friend in Jesus, he's everything to me, he's the fairest of ten thousand to my soul."

He watched them closely and settled in to listen to another long sermon, the price he paid to see her in clothes, that is, since he was dreaming about touching her body without clothes right under where he was sitting at that moment.

At the same time on Wednesday, she was waiting for him at the door. They walked down the steps, and this time she took the teacher's chair and directed him to sit in front of her.

They talked briefly about the village boy who had been hit by a car while riding his horse. He was in critical condition, and Ruth said that Thursday's prayer meeting would be focused on asking God to save the boy's life.

She then began to unbutton her blouse; he easily finished the last two. He stood in front of her and took her bra off.

She pushed him down gently and said, "Now it is your turn." She lifted his T-shirt off, stood, pulled him up, and hugged and held him.

"Relax," she told him as she slowly pushed him backward.

She stood over him, unbuckled his belt, and pulled off his jeans. Next came his underpants, and he immediately covered his penis with his hands. He was scared, inhibited, and well, everything had shrunk to the size of a mustard seed.

He didn't know what to do next. Ruth did.

First, she moved him to the horizontal position, same as she had taken the week before, covered him with a towel she had brought from home, and told him to breathe. She moved the towel over his body gently and then used her hands. He was a healthy seventeen-year-old, and soon his instincts took over.

She caught his ejaculation in the towel, wiped him down, and asked, "Are you okay?"

He thought he was paralyzed. She laughed and moved him back to vertical, looking straight into his eyes. Still bare breasted, she dressed him slowly.

Ruth understood that the minutes spent together in the Sunday School basement were not unlimited, and Burl's calm demeanor so far had given her the confidence to continue.

Likewise, he understood there were more eyes on her than on him and considered himself to be the luckiest boy in the town.

It was a dangerous secret they were living, and yet, in her mind, they could start having sex, make love, fuck. She didn't care what anyone called it. After all, God had given her *sangre caliente*. Now, in her quiet prayers, she thanked God for making Burl available to her.

So it went. They started having sexual intercourse. She bought a sleeping bag in Jacksonville and added a blanket and towel from home. She kept them rolled up in the church's office. They moved the tables together so they had room on the concrete floor. As she expected, he was nervous and awkward but calmed down by August, probably because football practice had started, and he was tired.

She showed him her "magic button" and urged him to touch it in as many ways as he could. To him, it was advice more important than any biblical commandment.

He learned to live two lives. One as the star quarterback and top student in his class with all the adult and classmate adulation that came with both. The other as a secret sex life with the married piano player in his church. And to continue their commandment game, Ruth had come up with an eleventh commandment, "Thou shall not be selfish with our partner," and then shortened it to "don't be selfish."

Burl knew he was lucky, had thanked God, eyes open, for sending him Ruth, and, unlike the confusing messages upstairs, he was eager to absorb the pleasure she gave him downstairs.

At the beginning of September, the Wabash Railroad needed a part-time bookkeeper at its village depot. It was no secret that Ruth did that kind of work well, so she took the job and started writing checks for the station workers. Unlike her volunteer work at the church, Wabash would pay her a fair wage.

Then on the last Wednesday of September, just after they had started to go downstairs, a loud knock sounded on the locked church door.

Ruth turned off the basement lights, whispered to Burl to hide downstairs, and walked slowly to the locked door. Standing on the front step was one-legged Webb Coffman who lived alone across the street from the church. He had knocked on the door with one of his homemade crutches and had a cigarette hanging from his mouth. The bank teller remembered that he had $241 in his checking account.

Webb had had his left leg blown off at Normandy and returned to the village as a broken hero. He was a salty village character; everyone knew him and he them. He ran the local pool hall, usually with a can of Stag beer in his hand and a Lucky Strike between his lips. More gin rummy was played than pool at Webb's Web.

He hated the government that sent him to war, hated the churches that promised life after death, and loved the St. Louis Cardinals. When they were playing, Harry Caray would be heard describing every play on KMOX in the Web.

"Ruth, Ruth, we need to talk."

"Webb, please, there is no smoking in the sanctuary."

In deference to her, not the church, he dropped and rubbed out his cigarette with his crutch tip.

Standing in front of her—she didn't invite him to sit in a pew—he said, "Now, for some time, I have watched Burl enter the church on Wednesday nights when you are here alone. You know me, Ruth, I don't give a shit what is going on between you two. I am guessing it is more about life than death. But if I see you, soon someone else will. That person would be less understanding than me and you would lose everything you have going here."

Looking straight at him—he was always unshaven and had terrible nicotine stains on his teeth—she said, "Right Webb. The time he spends here with me would be impossible to explain. My fault, I lost my be-careful focus this summer."

In a moment of levity, Webb looked around the church and laughingly said, "If there really was a God, Ruth, he or she would have been the one knocking on the door tonight. Instead, it was just me, your one-legged pool hall manager."

With that, he turned and crutched out the door and down the steps—stopping in the middle of the street to light a Lucky Strike—and crossed the dark street to his house.

Downstairs Burl and Ruth sat on two teacher chairs and discussed Webb's visit. She admitted to being needy, and it had made her careless for them both. She lamented that there was no back door to the building. Burl was keenly aware that he had nothing to lose, she everything.

"Let's pray," she said and took his hand and thanked God for Webb and asked for divine guidance in the next months of their lives. Burl kept his eyes open.

They decided not to meet for a while. Burl was in the middle of another undefeated football season and was being noticed statewide. The whole town, including Ruth and her husband, would attend the Friday night games, both home and away.

He was getting plenty of handkerchiefs dropped by junior and senior girls, but it was hard to take them seriously. None tempted him. He was in the middle of his season and missing his sexual lessons from a mature woman.

When Webb came into the bank to make his usual Friday deposit, Ruth had motioned him to her window and wrote an extra THANK YOU on his receipt. He acknowledged her message and mouthed, "Be careful." She was confident Webb would keep their secret.

Burl threw three touchdown passes in the team's final game to secure a second undefeated season in a row. Ruth was so proud of him that she and the other bank tellers did a cheer for him when he came to deposit his Wabash check. His reputation as the town's hero continued to grow.

From then until the spring hay season, he would study to keep his straight-A average and work at the roundhouse. He started taking his homework there to avoid his parents' increasing surveillance and complaints about his faithfulness. Plus, it saved him from having to go to the Thursday prayer meetings when, if he didn't have work, he pretended to have it. Of course, his parents enjoyed his football success but reminded him daily that *he knew what was right.*

Actually, I don't, he thought, but he could never say those words out loud. His time with Ruth had freed his mind in new ways and made it comfortable to question the church's spoon-fed answers. Learning about the woman's syrup was important and, well, what else was out there that he didn't know? Not one time did he think that their behavior was a sin. How could it be, since Ruth, being the good Christian woman that she was, had carried him across this bridge.

It was the first Sunday in December, and he was listening to them sing "Are Ye Able, Said the Master."

"Are ye able said the Master, to be crucified with me?"

He was thinking about the breasts inside Ruth's blouse. She'd given him her now-expected warm smile on the way to her seat. The dreaded sermon started, he was sitting with his parents, and he began to picture the location of the Wabash depot, its side door, the switching spurs in the rail yard in front of the roundhouse, and the size of the stall pits underneath the locomotives. He had gotten good at daydreaming through the nonsensical sermons.

Since Webb's visit, they knew her parked car and no back door exposed them too much. Her car parked among others in the Wabash lot would be normal and way better than just hers in front of the church. The depot had a back door on the dark side that opened to the switchyard spurs. The roundhouse door was in the back past the spur tracks.

He came to when they began to sing the get-saved song "Softly and Tenderly."

"Softly and tenderly Jesus is calling, calling for you and for me."

On the walk home, Burl continued to consider the merits of his plan. He was eager. Was she?

That Monday he finished his work quickly, walked outside, and counted the number of tracks from the depot's back door to the roundhouse. Beside the main east–west line, there were five spurs to walk over from the depot's door to the roundhouse. He decided to draw a diagram with a question mark and slip it to her during his next deposit at the bank.

As the days dragged toward Friday, he became more unsure of his plan but slid the note to her anyway. She looked at him with a question mark—he had given it to her upside down. Right side up to her, she smiled.

Ruth was desperate to reconnect with him. She had concluded that she sang better, was a better mother and wife, and was closer to God when they were having sex. She always carried Dr. Kay's revelation inside.

She considered Burl's drawing an answer to her prayers. It pleased her to know that he had taken the initiative to plan a solution for meetings.

That Sunday she sang "All the Way My Savior Leads Me."

"All the way my savior leads me; What have I to ask be-side? Can I doubt his tender mercy, who thru life has been my guide."

Afterward she drove by the depot and looked closely at how many tracks were between the depot and the roundhouse. She didn't know how dark the area was at night, but on Tuesday after she had completed the local payroll, she opened the back door and walked carefully across the rail yard and opened the backdoor of the roundhouse. She could see him up in stall three, wiping down the cab's windows on locomotive 931.

She climbed up the engine's ladder. They embraced without words and had sex in the engineer's seat. It had way more room than her car and was softer than the floor in the church basement.

She looked around at the inside of the roundhouse, always an amazing place for first timers, and said, "At least Webb can't crutch across the railroad tracks."

They laughed, and she began a short prayer thanking God for allowing them to enjoy their bodies again.

After they dressed, he walked her down the steps into the rectangular pit under 931. It was like a small underground room that came with steam-engine smells. It is where he had to wipe brake parts and check the sandbox that provided sand to help with friction at different times. It had two drop-cord lights at both ends and was four-by-ten-feet long. He thought it might be too scary for her.

She whistled and said, "This is bigger and more private than the church basement. Do you have a place to store our sleeping bag?"

So on it went for the next year and a half. He took one girl to homecoming and another to prom. Both were eager to have sex, and he accommodated them. Neither came close to the pleasure he felt with Ruth. He offered no opinions at nightly laundromat committee meetings, and they began to tease him about being queer. He just didn't show any interest in the schoolgirls.

She taught him the many ways a farmers' bank made money. He discussed his football team and wondered why they were drafting so many tenant farm kids to go fight in Vietnam. Sometimes they would just meet and talk, down in the tomb below a locomotive. They had become close friends. Ruth had become his rock in more ways than he understood.

Ruth was so much easier to talk to than his parents. Burl was so full of life and hope that it made her feel young again.

Yet each accepted their unique life position and understood that their secret liaisons would end when he graduated and left town.

Since their Webb warning, Ruth was vigilant to not risk their secret times and was constantly on guard to avoid being seen walking across the tracks at night by a townsperson. The deal she had made with her body had canceled any concern that God was watching. He could monitor all the rest, but her body was off-limits.

They discussed Burl's waning interest in God, laughed at themselves and each other and enjoyed honest sex, usually beneath a six-hundred-ton locomotive. Ruth always believed that God had answered her prayers. Burl wondered, sometimes out loud to her, what the difference was between God's answering prayer and luck. Until he left for college, Ruth lobbied that God answered prayers.

The town hero left to play football two states away. It was not a lovers' breakup, but a more painful separation than anticipated. They had been enjoying sweet pleasure physically and mentally for two years. Then nothing.

It took Burl two years to push his Ruth rock behind him and enjoy time with girls his age. Ruth began accepting invitations to sing all over the state just to get out of town. The recognition she received did not come close to filling her void.

Menopause came early, and she asked God, "Why?"

Forty years went by.

Over the years Ruth's singing was noticed by a regional television station, and she became a highly paid star on the evangelical circuit. She quit her job at the bank and depot and was often asked to sign autographs after her television performances.

In a squabble with the local pastor, she and her husband left the Southern Baptist Church and built their own, the New Song Tabernacle. They and other singers built a church and saved more souls than any other in the region.

She remained celibate the rest of her life and shunned all the evangelists' one-night-stand offers. She had been the one to initiate the sweet years with Burl, and none of the preachers tempted her in the least.

Webb Coffman was run over while crossing Route 100 by a grain truck that had lost its brakes driving through town. It happened in front of the bank, and Ruth saw it all.

Tom died of a sudden heart attack, and she remained in their village home.

Burl had a mediocre quarterback career at the university; there were too many players, and the field was too long.

He had a stellar academic record, was the class president, and was always on the dean's list. It disappointed him that he was smarter than he was a good football player.

He avoided the Vietnam War draft and went to Canada. He didn't know anyone in Vietnam, and they didn't know him. The town hero instantly became an unpatriotic draft dodger. It pleased Ruth, though, and she always thanked God for his bold decision.

He enjoyed many sexual liaisons and always made sure he followed Ruth's eleventh commandment. He married a Creole woman from Montreal, and they had two brown children.

He taught and researched neuropsychology at Memorial University in St. John's Newfoundland.

The steam locomotive was replaced by the diesel engine. Better than the locomotive, it could push and pull equally and didn't need a roundhouse, which became the town's haunted house and was then demolished.

Burl had returned off and on through the years, burying his father and then his mother, but had never been able to connect with Ruth in private. During those times they would see each other, but there were always too many people around for them to touch each other as they wanted to. Each could see it in the other's eyes.

He had been asked to return to help bury a favorite class-mate and, on the way there, realized it had been forty years since he and Ruth had talked privately. Considering their different trajectories, he became overwhelmed with gratitude and decided he *had* to talk to her this visit, no matter what. The more he thought about the forty years, the more embar-rassed and ashamed he became that he hadn't gone to her.

He knocked on her door at 10 a.m. He knew she would be alone. Now seventy-seven, she smiled at him, took his hand, and led him into her living room. He remembered her leading him to the church basement. She sat him down on the couch and moved her rocking chair directly in front of him, still holding his hand. Then she sat down and covered her legs with the same sleeping bag they'd used in the church basement and roundhouse.

He was nervous, but his hands were not shaking. Ruth started to cry softly.

He said, "I wanted to thank you for being the most important person in my life. You coached me so much in those years and I want to make sure you know how grateful I am."

"Huh? What are you talking about, Burl? I loved you." He was speechless.

Tears were now streaming down her face. And his. He reached over, grabbed a tissue, and wiped her eyes gently. He then took her hands, lifted her up, and hugged her completely. With her chin on his shoulder, she began to whisper a prayer in his ear.

This time, he closed his eyes.

Eat Your Heart Out, Bob Knight, You'll Never Have a Win Like This*

When I was selected to coach Antigua's national basketball team in the 1982 Caricom Tournament in Jamaica, there was a lot less hoopla than when Bob Knight was chosen to coach the 1984 U.S. Olympic basketball team. A committee of experts had picked Knight because he was the best college coach at that time. Meanwhile, I was chosen by the island's officials because I loved their calypso music.

I had not coached two NCAA championship teams, nor had I devised strategies that have universally affected the game, nor was I was on Puerto Rico's most-wanted list—that was Bob Knight. Often referred to as the *General*, Knight never tolerated people calling him *Bobby*. If you did, he would pounce on you like a hungry lion and eat you on the spot, in front of everyone.

I did admire Coach Knight for the innovative tactics he contributed to the game but not his crude, egomaniac style of always turning the spotlight on himself. I had heard him speak at clinics and I knew we were not cut from the same cloth.

---

* First published in the November 5, 1984, edition of *Sports Illustrated*.

I was an unknown, thirty-eight-year-old, small college coach at Oakland University in Michigan. But the Antiguans had a passing acquaintance with me because our team had traveled there on a Christmas tour in 1979. They wanted an American coach, Bob already had his assignment, and I was offered the job.

Other than psychic income, no pay went with it, which was fine by me. It was a deal I couldn't refuse—round-trip airfare and room and board for three weeks in Antigua. Since the average weekly Antiguan wage was around sixty dollars, I knew they were serious about their basketball.

I flew to Saint John's, Antigua, on August 1, 1982, to mold their twelve best players into a team that could compete with the Bahamas, Dominica, Trinidad, Suriname, and Jamaica, the defending Caricom champion. As I settled into my seat on Eastern Airlines Flight 963, I realized that I was more excited to go to Antigua than I would be to go to LA for the 1984 Olympics. It wasn't an actual rationalization, you see, I'm an island boy by heart.

Antigua is a three-hour flight from Miami. It's twice as big as Manhattan, has 365 beaches—one for every day of the year and has approximately 80,000 citizens. Antiguans swear they invented calypso and declare a Calypso King at their annual Carnival celebration.

I stayed with my host, Lucaso Brumant, in the capital of St. John's. He was an official of their government's department of sports and games, taught part-time at Christ the King elementary school, and was involved in everything about basketball on the island. Lucaso was best man at my wedding in Antigua and I was his in Georgetown, Guyana. We remain lifelong friends.

I had just fourteen days to prepare my team for the

tournament that was to be played in Kingston, Jamaica. The average age of my players was twenty-one. They worked as longshoremen, musicians, cabinetmakers, and mechanics, among other occupations. Each had a unique, memorable quality.

One of my best players, Richie Francis, wore a diamond earring, which was new to me as a coach. Bum, an older but skilled guard, liked to smoke marijuana before, after, and during practice. Grantley Samuels, who was built like a cement mixer, wore a baseball cap with the bill turned up during practice and play. Canya, a Rastafarian, had dreadlocks down to his butt and sometimes, but not always, tied them up in a bundle.

Tekal Gomes, our six-foot-ten center, was always an hour late for practice.

One of my favorites, Nya, sometimes played barefoot, and if he did wear shoes, he wouldn't wear socks. Bobby Joseph was always thirty minutes early for practice and a delight to coach because of his great attitude. Wyllie Abbott was a soft-spoken bank clerk and ultimately surprised everyone by becoming our team's best player in Jamaica.

The Christian brothers, Mark and Andy, were known more for their soccer than basketball talents, but I had to have them on our team because everyone on the island knew and loved them. Their father ran the biggest grocery store in Saint John's, and Mark and Andy had worked there since they could walk.

Like all island people, my players were proud of their country and excited for the opportunity to play for Antigua. Because the island is so small and has no interscholastic or collegiate competition, playing on the national team was front-page, headline news. It was easy for me to adopt their feelings. I just wanted to coach them into a team. This would prove not to be an easy task.

The team and I practiced outdoors under poor lighting on pot-holed asphalt since there was no indoor court on the island. The court was located in "down Villa," which was a neighborhood grazing area for cows and goats.

More serious than constantly dealing with cow pies on the court was the fact that my players were not used to coaching. My being a white guy and giving coaching corrections to a team of individuals who had never been coached didn't go anywhere close to smoothly. At best, the team's style was chaotic and random, and it did not include passing the ball to a teammate.

So, there I was with a group of island boys who thought nothing of being late, smoking a doobie on the way to practice, and not passing the ball. I laughed out loud when I wondered what Bob Knight would do in this situation—he was a severe disciplinarian and famous for his sledgehammer style.

Instead, I chose to use the velvet hammer.

I put in three man-to-man plays and a simple zone offense and emphasized how good it felt to pass and receive one from a teammate. Luckily, I also put in the then-popular four-corners offense in which four players stand in the corners of the half court and the fastest dribbler goes for it.

We made progress in the first week and I even started taking a drag off Bum's doobie after practice just to prove I was not a Bob Knight wannabe. The players saw immediately that I was a novice and proceeded to coach me. We had big laughs and started coming together as a team.

Soon I was informed that the country's deputy prime minister, the honorable Lester Bird, wanted to meet me. At our high-level government meeting on a Saturday morning at his house, he received me in his underwear and shared the novel reason Antigua needed a basketball coach.

Bird felt the game's popularity had grown so fast since its introduction in the 1960s that it had become a positive factor in limiting illegitimate births among young people. Now I've heard many banquet speakers exalt the values of playing basketball, but this was a justification I'd never heard.

For our eleventh practice, my host, Lucaso, set up a public scrimmage so that I could see how our team would react under game conditions. We drove twenty minutes from St. John's to Cedar Grove, where junior teams from these communities would be playing the preliminary game. Our game against the rest of the best island players was to follow as the main event.

I hadn't realized that we had entered enemy territory, but I soon noticed that the country players were beating the hell out of the city team, and their mood was so hostile that the city team quit in the third quarter. I'd never seen a team walk off the court like that, and I was dumbfounded.

Lucaso started arguing with two local officials. The Cedar Grove team, joined by several country comrades, took combative positions on the court. For a reason I didn't know then, they were determined to prevent us from playing our game.

Our players began to line up to shoot practice lay-ups. There was some pushing and shoving, and as Andy Christian prepared to shoot our first lay-up, a man with a canoe paddle stepped out and said, "Don't come any farther."

Built like a Sherman tank, Andy accepted the dare.

As Andy rose to shoot, the man hit him across the shoulders with the paddle. It shattered like a clay pigeon. Andy threw his attacker to the ground. The country boy got up, ran out, and returned with a chunk of concrete the size of a football. This time, Andy ran. His aggressor caught up with him and hurled the concrete missile. Andy leaped like a hurdler and was hit in the shoulder. Any normal human would have collapsed on the spot—not Andy. Hard as a rock himself, he landed on his feet, picked up the chunk, and took off after his assailant.

Meanwhile, other Cedar Grovers had picked up rocks and surrounded our team. We were like a matador in the bull-fighting ring and the bulls were clawing the dirt with their hoofs. Suddenly, I watched Tekal take a direct hit on the knee from point-blank range. Mark Christian was struck in the back of the head.

When a chunk whistled past my ear, in one of my more brilliant moments ever, I said, "Let's get the hell out of here!"

We helped our wounded as we all literally ran for our lives. A mile out of town, Lucaso picked us up in the van. He then proceeded to explain the reason for the debacle. The Cedar Grove players felt that Lucaso had cheated them the week before when he refereed a game of theirs in St. John's. They were convinced his favoritism was the reason they'd lost to an inferior city team.

Me? I couldn't have asked for a more emotional event to bring my guys together.

The next day we found out that the Caricom Tournament had been postponed indefinitely because of a polio outbreak in Jamaica. We were all terribly disappointed. Even before our harrowing experience in Cedar Grove, I had felt we were ready to compete as a team. Now we were all revved up with no place to go.

Disappointed, I returned home to Michigan in mid-August and made arrangements for barefoot Nya to enroll at Michigan Christian College and Mark Christian to play soc-cer at Oakland. We settled into our respective challenges and waited for the tournament to be rescheduled. On December 14, I got word that the tournament in Jamaica was back on. Our first game would be against Trinidad in just two days.

Mark, Nya, and I caught the first available flight from Detroit to Montego Bay on December 16, the opening day of the tournament. From there we were to take a bus to Kingston to rendezvous with the rest of the team, which had flown from Antigua with Lucaso.

I was the seventeenth person to get into our twelve-passenger van. We peeled out of Montego Bay and catapulted our way up, down, and around the ribbons the Jamaicans call roads. We finally arrived, forty minutes late. I was in no shape to make my debut as a famous international basketball coach. We walked into the arena with ten seconds left in the first half and our team behind by one point. I asked Lucaso lots of questions and then coached them to a twelve-point loss.

Actually, we did pretty well, considering the condition in which I found the team. Lucaso had left Tekal behind because he hadn't come to practice since August. During my absence, a local coach had put in a strange offense, dropping mine. It seemed to be designed for a man-to-man defense, which might have worked if Trinidad hadn't played a zone.

My most serious problem, however, was that the players who had remained in Antigua were jealous of those I'd taken to the states. The stay-behinds felt slighted and were determined to make life miserable for Nya, Mark, and me.

We had two more games left in our pool to see who'd play in the championship game. We were scheduled to play Dominica in two days, a team we were supposed to beat. We practiced twice a day, and I tried to solve my problems with Tekal's absence, no real center, a strange new offense, and lots of dissension.

We lost to Dominica by ten points. Any coaching I tried fell on deaf ears. However, the crazy tournament schedule resulted in us having to play the final game against Jamaica, the defending champions and host. The arena would be sold out, we were the patsies, and of course, the home team would win, and Jamaica would celebrate.

The Jamaican team seemed invincible. They had men with NBA size and their best player was called Skywalker for obvious reasons. It would be a miracle if we came close—any stateside bookie would have us as thirty-point underdogs.

The day before the final, Lucaso gave a heartrending speech to the team and me. He told us how he had put himself on the line with the government to get money for the trip. He reminded the guys about the love they have for the mother country, and he made it clear that we had to make an honorable showing or, frankly, he would be too embarrassed to go home and face his superiors.

I worked hard with the team. We began to have better practices, mostly because the players realized I wouldn't quit on them. I played Bum and Grantley more, Nya and Mark less.

When the game started, the arena was packed with Jamaicans, ready to beat up on lowly Antigua and party afterward. As I'd anticipated, their team tried to get the ball inside. But we clogged up the lane and made them shoot from the perimeter. When they missed, they played volleyball with the basketball until they scored. But we were scoring too and were only eight points down at the half.

Jamaica scored two quick baskets to start the second half. Then, a miracle began to unfold. During the next eight minutes, we outscored them thirty to four. They called their last time-out with nine minutes left in the game. We were ahead by fourteen points! We were riding this monstrous wave of momentum and were as bewildered as the Jamaicans in the stands.

Their coach wisely changed from a zone to a man-to-man defense. Since I had thrown out the appropriate offense, we started having trouble scoring. Losing our lead fast, at 4:32 minutes remaining, I called our last time-out. We were five points ahead and now panicking.

"Remember the four corners offense we practiced in St. John's?"

No player offered a "yes," so I walked them out on the court, assigned a player a corner, and told Nya to dribble around and make something happen, all in front of the laughing Jamaican fans.

During the four minutes, Nya and Wyllie each scored a basket and the Jamaicans scored seven points. We were up by two.

By this time, the Jamaican referees had given in to the screaming crowd and began to call everything in the local team's favor. With thirty-two seconds left, Skywalker made two free throws to tie the score.

The next scene, however, will live forever in my memory and surely in the memories of all those who played and watched.

We get the ball inbounds.
Nya dribbles around for twelve seconds and shoots a wild shot.
There's a mad scramble with bodies flying everywhere.
The ball is flicked loose and bounces out in the lane.
Grantley roars out of the pack, picks up the ball, and rainbows it toward the basket.

Nothing but net!
The Jamaicans attack our zone for one last shot.
They set up . . . and Bum makes the interception.
We win!
The crowd and refs are stunned, their postgame victory celebration canceled.
We are hysterical.
All the other tournament teams come out of the stands and carry our players around like heroes.
Lucaso and I hug each other with tears streaming down our faces.

Lucaso, the team, and I stayed out all night. We drank Red Stripe beer, laughed, and sang the chorus repeatedly from Antiguan King Short Shirt's new song "Press On": *Sometimes it seems justice is really blind, those who are wrong live right, press on, Press on, don't give up, don't give up, Don't give up!* which turned out to be good training for me. You see, in January 1983, the government made me an honorary citizen. Eat your heart out, Bobby.

Note: Bob Knight died November 3, 2023. The author's first in-person experience with Knight was as a Bradley University basketball player when Bradley played Army in the 1964 National Invitational Tournament at Madison Square Garden. Knight was the assistant coach. The two crossed paths again in the summer of 1985 at a basketball clinic in Deland, Florida, where Knight congratulated the author and said, "Not for the story, but for being able to put up with the island ways."

A Taste of Curry

Suriname?

When he first heard that word, Ran was coaching the Antiguan national basketball team at the 1982 Caribbean Community Tournament in Kingston, Jamaica. Embarrassed he had never heard of the country and wanting to learn more, he was drawn to the Surinamese team, also playing in the tournament, and the news about what had occurred in their country five days before their arrival in Jamaica.

What he learned was horrifying. In a coup d'état, General Desi Bouterse's soldiers had murdered fifteen journalists, teachers, and lawyers. The team members knew many of the victims and soldiers; some were family. Suriname was under curfew and the group feared what would happen next.

Because the Surinamese and Antiguans shared a dormitory floor, Ran politely walked through their privacy curtain across the hall and became an accepted participant in their discussions. He was intrigued by their stories and amazed that he was talking to people from a country led by a dictator.

On the other hand, since the United States was considered the Mecca of basketball, they wanted to learn how to conduct practices, how to teach zone presses, and how to design an offense. Ran and the coaches became fast friends.

With their minds on the uncertainty at home, the Surinamese team played poorly during the week of games. The morning of their last game, a military officer from Suriname entered the dormitory and ordered them to immediately pack their bags and get on the bus outside.

They would be returning on the military plane he had arrived on an hour before. "The general is disappointed in your performance here and you are wasting his money," he told them.

Downcast, the coaches and players quickly tossed their possessions into their bags.

Over the course of the week, some of the Surinamese players and coaches had asked Ran if he could help them stay in Jamaica or maybe get them to the United States, but their premature departure did not allow for further discussion or planning. Ran forced his way onto the bus before it departed to wish the men good luck. The team captain stood to give Ran a Suriname jersey and the whole team clapped.

He clapped back at them and wished them good luck. The emotional vaccination this experience gave him would take and Suriname would stay with him for the rest of his life.

Ran's team from the little island won the tournament and the Antiguans returned home national heroes. He went back to coach his NCAA team, which had thirteen games left on its schedule. Of course, these games were important, but he had Suriname on his mind and kept up-to-date with the happenings there, mostly through phone calls and airmail.

Seven months later, when Ran got an invitation to fly to Suriname to share his ideas on how to get college scholarships and conduct clinics for Surinamese players, he was thrilled. The Surinamese believed Americans knew everything about basketball, so their coaches convinced General Bouterse to pay Ran's expenses to visit. It helped, too, that basketball was the dictator's favorite sport.

Ran was pleased to get the invite from a country no one knew about. He preferred to make his friends uncomfortable with statements like "I'd rather go to Paramaribo than Paris," and "Their country is run by a dictator who has killed people."

A month after the invitation, Ran arrived in Paramaribo on Suriname Airways and was escorted off the plane to the airport's VIP room by sweaty, smelly soldiers armed with AK-47s. Ran surmised that deodorant was not a standard issue in their barracks despite the ninety-degree temperatures and high humidity. It smelled like there were no showers at headquarters either.

The basketball officials he'd become acquainted with months earlier in Jamaica greeted him in the air-conditioned VIP room. They reviewed his schedule of meetings and official appearances all culminating in an official government dinner on Friday night and a basketball party at the federation president's house on Sunday evening.

Afterward, they drove him to the Voss Officer's Club in the middle of Paramaribo, a single-story complex with twelve overnight rooms, and a restaurant with a spacious seating area. It also had a fifty-meter swimming pool that made Ran smile; he was a lap swimmer back home.

Before Ran and the officials got out of the car, they quietly warned him that the general often went to Voss for meetings with his armed entourage.

"He trusts no one, especially Americans, but he loves basketball, and he paid for your air ticket," they reminded him.

Ran trudged through the week of perfunctory meetings, mostly playing the role as exhibit A, the American expert. He put on clinics for the country's basketball coaches and trained the national team twice. Ran loved this work.

During his second clinic with youth coaches conducted at Voss, General Desi Bouterse had entered the room and walked straight up to Ran as he was drawing a play on the chalkboard. The room became instantly quiet.

The general held his hand out to Ran and said, "Thanks for coming to Suriname, our coaches speak highly of you. We'll talk later."

As Ran watched Bouterse walk out the room, he was surprised at how short the dictator was. *A small point guard maybe*, he thought. He turned to the room of coaches and the disdain in the room for Bouterse was palpable.

By the third day, it dawned on him that his visit was giving legitimacy to the military government. There were too many men standing on corners with machine guns for him and naively he wondered what the soldiers were afraid of.

Whenever he could escape Henke, his host and assistant secretary of state, and the government car, he walked the streets of Paramaribo and sat on a bench in the centrum, usually on Tammenga Straat, and would just smile in awe. There were so many different colors of people and so many languages spoken that he felt he was at a world bazaar of humans. Compared to looking through a monocular back home, the Surinamese mix was as eye-popping as looking through a kaleidoscope.

Dinner that Friday evening was staged in a Javanese restaurant where they shared a variety of curries with different types of meat, rice, and Java Beer. Until that night, curry had never touched Ran's forty-year-old lips, but he was game to them all, green, yellow, brown, and red. Some dishes were more picante than others, and the rice was unfriendly, light and fluffy, not sticky. He discovered that he favored the yellow curry prepared with coconut milk.

Like the food, the beer had different spice profiles. It looked and foamed like Budweiser, but it contained no alcohol. Not a big drinker, he enjoyed the taste and didn't miss the alcohol.

The three-hour dinner turned his tongue into a trampoline. His taste buds were doing somersaults trying to differentiate between the new flavors and aromas, when Henke leaned across the table and declared, "Let's go get dessert!"

Ran assumed they would return to Voss.

Instead, they pulled into the VIP parking lot of the Condor Night Club where Henke asked, "Do you like to fuck with romance or without?"

Ran opened his mouth to say *"romance,"* but Henke quickly said, "Don't worry, let's go! I'll introduce you to my favorites. The government is buying."

As they entered the Condor Club, Ran took a deep breath and relaxed. He had experience in this kind of place and knew how to proceed in a way that wouldn't make Henke suspicious.

He could practice what he had learned while working on a merchant marine ship.

Between semesters back when Ran was a college student, he had worked as a deckhand on the Norwegian freighter *MS Santos,* which sailed between New York City and Buenos Aires. There he had experienced firsthand the ugly world of seamen's brothels where the working women were abused and often beaten black-and-blue.

Out to his first house in Recife, Brazil, with his deck crewmates, he had been shocked and confused when the woman he had chosen undressed. He felt sorry for her; he wanted to treat her kindly. During the rest of his trip, he would choose a woman at each port, talk with her and listen to her story, touch her compassionately, and pay twice the going rate. And sometimes, when he felt the attraction was genuinely mutual, he did enjoy sex with them. The women's stories stayed with him more than anything he had learned during his four years at the university.

Inside the Condor Club, Ran had asked the greeting group of girls where they were from and how old they were. Lula had quickly answered, "I'm from Kenya and I am twenty-eight years old." Passing his English test because he would want to talk to her, he quickly chose her.

Inside the small room, he assured her he would pay her extra, but they had to keep their voices low while they talked since the walls of the room didn't reach the ceiling.

Lula's skin was ebony, yet Ran could still see the bruises on her neck and body, bluish ones from more recent encounters and yellow ones from days before. She told him she had been a "working" girl from age sixteen and that her real name was Anisa.

Like all the young women he had met in the same situation, she was confused by this man who was curious about her life. Besides English, Ran learned Lula spoke Swahili, Spanish, and Dutch. From his experience on the ship, he knew being multilingual was normal for women in the profession. Lula told him the story of how she had ended up in Paramaribo and, feeling safe in his presence, fell asleep.

Ran listened to the primordial sounds of brothel sex and to Lula's snoring. When Henke signaled it was time to leave, Ran woke Lula so they could walk out together, and Lula could give Henke the thumbs-up.

Friday night's dessert is over, Ran thought. *Mission accomplished.*

The next morning in the shower, Ran shook his head at himself as he reviewed the previous night's events. He had long ago given up searching for the answer to why some men beat women and some did not. It had become a shoulder-shrug conflict since his deckhand days; he had no answers, an increasing trend in his life.

The women's stories were eerily the same. A sequence of terrible luck pushed them out of their homes, their bodies the only way to earn money. And, if they had the capacity, the more languages they learned, the more clients they could attract.

They had no hope and were trapped with little opportunity to change the courses of their lives. He had wished last night, as he had on the ship, that things weren't this way. But they were. Ran knew he didn't have the power to change their trajectories.

Ran pushed this sadness aside. It was Saturday morning, his first day free from meetings and being driven around by government officials who were always drinking their own bathwater. Being with his basketball coaching friends was where he wanted to be, but Henke used Ran mostly for the government's benefit. Being hosted required him to be their pet rabbit, but now he had until Sunday night to relax and explore on his own.

He had made plans to visit the Central Market, and now with the mysteries of the curry flavors still lingering on his tongue, he would be on a very important mission.

Hell, he thought, *it took me forty years before I tasted curry, what the hell is it?*

As he walked to the barracks' exit to catch a local cab, he saw that the guard had stopped a woman at the entry gate.

There was a loud exchange and a second guard approached. That's when he recognized her.

"Lula?"

She was wearing a yellow sundress and a scarf around her neck, both covering the bruises he had seen the night before. In daylight and without fuck-me makeup, *Anisa* bore no resemblance to Lula.

As naturally as he could, Ran greeted her and told the guards, "She is escorting me this morning to the Central Market; Henke is off duty today."

The scene was robust with conflict. Voss was the officers club where General Desi Bouterse, Suriname's military dictator, held frequent meetings. Two days before, Ran had met him briefly, shook his hand, but had not talked to him.

The guards were not sure what to do with the odd couple standing in front of them at ten in the morning; after all, it was a secure military base. Noting their hesitation, Ran grabbed Anisa's arm and boldly walked out of the gate. The pair got into a taxi, but she was obviously uncomfortable.

She turned to him and said, "I'm sorry if I embarrassed you. I knew you would be here because Voss is where the government puts their VIP guests, and they often bring them to the club. Of course, my name was not on the pass list, but here I am to say thank you for treating me nicely last night. Let me get out of the taxi now. I can walk back."

"No, no, you'll come to the market with me," Ran said, not fully understanding her reluctance.

She shook her head. "We can't go to the market together. You are bigshot American . . . and white. I am black . . . a lady of the night from Kenya. The women in the market will dismiss us because we will be out in the open in the middle of the day. Our being together in broad daylight is taboo here.

"If given the chance, Henke will use any gossip against you. You know he's the deputy secretary of state, don't you? I only wanted to thank you for being kind to me."

"Do you *want* to go with me?" Ran asked.

Anisa bowed her head and whispered, "I've never been inside the market before."

"Your voice is lower today," he observed. "Last night it came from here." He touched her lips with his fingertips.

"Today it is here," he said as he touched her chest between her braless breasts.

She smiled. "That's right. We use at least two voices. You know Ran, we are actresses. First, we must *catch* them with our sexy voices and red lipstick, and then we must get them in and out fast if you know what I mean."

Ran nodded. He knew too well.

While watching the houses zip by out the taxi's window, Ran acknowledged to the passersby that he was sitting next to a woman who spoke four languages plus her professional voice; he spoke one.

Soon, two first-time visitors, covering opposite poles of skin color and violating the local rules, walked into the teeming Central Market on the banks of the Suriname River. Ran felt the immediate disapproval, especially from the women vendors, but he forged ahead with Anisa by his side.

The market was crowded with customers and vendors alike. Nationalities ranged from Surinamese Maroons, East Indians, and Chinese to Amerindians, Lebanese, Brazilians, Javanese, and some white people, mostly Dutch, Ran assumed. They were all laughing and talking in as many languages as there were skin colors, that is, until Ran and Anisa walked up to look at the wares and perhaps buy something.

When Ran ordered cups of fresh mango-pineapple juice,

Anisa's was only half full. He immediately exchanged his full cup with her and shook his head at the vendor. The homemade medicine oil, lotion, and cooking essence lady wasn't interested in explaining what was in the secondhand bottles she was hawking to them. And when he wanted to buy Anisa a necklace and asked the Brazilian artisan if she could try some on, the vendor doubled the price in front of him and offered only two to choose from.

Losing it, albeit briefly, Ran machine-gunned a few choice words at the Brazilian. Anisa pulled him away.

"It is me they despise," she told him, "because I remind them where their husbands go for fun. Guess who pays? All these women know, they just don't want to be reminded at the market on Saturday morning."

Scratching his head, he asked, "How do they know? You could be a bush negro, a Brazilian, the wife of Uganda's ambassador. I could be the Dutch ambassador."

As she pulled him out the nearest door and onto the street, Anisa answered, "You and I are not from here. They know. They *always* know. It's bigger than you and me. They have *their own history here*, and you are not dialed in to their frequency. Best to do some homework before you come to a place like Suriname."

Ran turned Anisa toward him and placed his hands gently on her shoulders. "You are an amazing woman and way smarter than me," he said. "Thank you for coming to Voss this morning."

She took his hand from her shoulder and squeezed it affectionately. "Please, let's get lunch. I'm hungry, and the kiosks outside will gladly take your money."

In charge now, Anisa ordered a roti with curried chicken for each of them, pineapple and mango juice in cups, and small pastries for dessert. This time their cups were filled equally. Food in hand, they walked to Revo Plein Park and sat under a banyan tree.

Ran was embarrassed for her, mad at the market vendors, and of course, pissed at himself for his ignorance. As they ate, he apologized for embarrassing her.

Anisa tried to soothe him. "None of us here are equal and each group is always trying to claw its way to the top of the "'I am better than you'" heap. These vendors and their unique community inside are on top today, working for their families. I will be on top tonight at the club with their bored husbands. And you have your own group here, having been invited by this government."

With those words, Anisa rose and announced her departure. He stood up as well and Anisa hugged him. "Look," she said, "I am going to Curacao tomorrow. It is too stressful here after the murders. Curacao is supposed to be safer, and it is a smaller country. Thank you, Ran, for letting me spend time with you today."

Sitting alone and watching her yellow dress get fainter as she walked away from him, he arranged her five words in a way he could incorporate them into a simple phrase: *"History didn't begin with you."*

Before this encounter with Anisa, he would acknowledge that his sensitivity to what had transpired before him was secondary to his arrival on the scene, any scene. He suffered from a self-important ego that often blew up in his face.

But witnessing Anisa's educated sensitivity of what was happening in front of them, and he hadn't, humbled his view of himself at that moment. "Okay, I am not important, so from now on, pay attention and dial the right frequency," he said to the banyan tree.

Accepting his good fortune to learn from an educated Kenyan woman in Paramaribo, he returned to the curry section of the market.

At the curry tables, ten women of all colors, sizes, and ages sold their own signature curry powder. Ran was equally interested in watching the various customers as they would go directly to the vendor selling their favorite blend, exchange money, and then leave as if buying a dime bag of cocaine on a street corner.

Ran people-watched in awe of the many colors of skin as he inhaled the combined aromas of mustard seed, tamarind, coriander, turmeric, cumin, hing, chiles, mehti, and ginger. He thought his brain would explode with the sensations entering his eyes and nose.

He wanted to sit down and ask each vendor how and why her blend was different from the others, but before he could make his move, a small group of Brazilian tourists wearing name tags descended upon him and the curry tables. He watched them roll their eyes in ecstasy as they sniffed the various spice mixtures.

Their tour guide was a young, petite Indian woman who spoke soft Portuguese and was obviously explaining the varieties of local curries. Her voice stopped him cold. The words from her lips hung suspended in the air and sparkled.

Long aware that a woman's voice attracted him first, her voice took a front-row seat in his hippocampus, pushing his sense of smell and sight to the back pews. He asked himself, *"Now what?"*

Temporarily paralyzed, Ran watched her exquisite gestures glide through the air as she gracefully manipulated the group away from the tables to another area of the market. For a moment, he was tempted to join the group just to listen more, but their departure left an opening at the tables for him to step in, ask about the mixtures, and make some purchases.

To the curry ladies, he was a white-guy-novelty to impress. That he was an American and not Dutch made him even more welcome. One woman spoke English, so she bridged the gap for the rest. There were basically four premixed varieties: red, yellow, green, and brown. Then there were variations of *how* red, *how* brown, and so on. Ran realized he didn't need a language interpreter when his nose did the translations. He spent an hour with them and bought eight bags, all different colors.

Wobbly and high from the tantalizing aromas, he took off through the market in search of the petite tour guide.

"Try not to embarrass yourself any more today, you fucking idiot," he scolded himself.

He stopped at an outside kiosk, bought a rose milk slush with coconut, a drink he had learned to love during the week, and began his walk back to Voss.

Along the way, with the *history* phrase front and center in his brain, he thought about Anisa's story and how lucky he was to have spent time with her. Ran had a master's degree in social science; she had a PhD in life.

Then there was the petite tour guide with the golden voice and, well, what about the guy carrying eight bags of magic curry back to Voss? Who was he? *A work in progress at best*, Ran thought as he turned into the barracks.

Ran got up early Sunday morning, took a swim in the Voss pool, and then dried on the deck as the sun rose from the east. He looked up into the trees surrounding the complex and saw at least three species of brightly colored parrots.

He mused to himself what a paradoxical country Suriname was, populated by gorgeous people of all colors, mixed like the spices in the amazing curries at the market, and ruled by a military dictator now eating breakfast about seventy-five yards from where he was sat.

He knew this because there were two soldiers with AK-47s standing guard at the entry door up the walk toward the restaurant.

Ran considered walking in and introducing himself to the general, but he remembered the defiant look on the coaches' faces when Bouterse had interrupted their clinic session. Ran was on the coaches' side, so he stayed put.

Eventually he got up and walked to Paramaribo's centrum and sat on the banks of the Suriname River. Before his trip, Ran had read that the slave ships from Africa used the river and city to renew supplies on their way to North America.

It was there that the desperate, non-swimming slaves would try to escape by jumping into the river full of piranhas. His emotions overcame him as he imagined the suffering and pain that occurred right in front of him. He took solace in knowing that some did escape into the jungle and became a respected group known as Bush Negroes.

The neighborhood party had been described as just a regular Sunday evening get-together of the basketball community in Paramaribo. When he arrived at the federation president's house, there were at least twenty-five people in the yard. Everyone spoke the local patois that was a blend of French, Dutch, Spanish, English, and Portuguese.

It was a lovely Sunday night, seventy-five degrees and lower than normal humidity; the music was sweet, and the coaches made him feel like he was one of them.

"Welcome!" the host, Stappie, declared when he saw him. "Drinks and food are in the kitchen, down the hall and to your left. Help yourself. My mother and our friend Cynthia are in charge."

When Ran turned that corner, the lovely Brazilian guide from the day before looked up from behind the kitchen table. He squeaked at the sight of her. At a loss for words, he blushed in painful embarrassment.

He retreated backward into the hall and took a slow walk around the yard to reclaim his voice. He chatted with the coaches he had met during the week and eventually headed back down the hall, his heart beating wildly.

He entered the kitchen and immediately went to the host's mother, held out his hand, and said, "Thank you for inviting me tonight. Your son has taken so much of his time to teach me about Suriname this week. I feel honored to call him a friend!"

The woman thanked him and kissed him on the cheek before returning to her hosting duties.

Ran then turned toward the petite Indian woman who was staring at him.

"I saw you yesterday at the market. You were leading a group," he said. "You were speaking Portuguese. You must be Cynthia, I'm Ran."

"Yes, we saw you," she said flatly, ignoring his introduction. "You are the American with a woman from the Condor Club who cursed at the jewelry vendor."

In two short sentences, she had pinned him against the wall. Her dark eyes pierced straight through him.

"You are right," he replied. "Anisa and I broke a few local rules, but we survived."

Cynthia rolled her eyes, handed him a Parbo beer, and coldly dismissed him by turning her back.

The thought of engaging Cynthia further, as intimidating as she was at all of one hundred pounds and standing five feet, two inches, made him dizzy. He was the kind of person who would accept such challenges; even though she had insulted him, he was confident that given time, he could change her opinion of him.

He asked the party's host about her and learned that she worked at the Brazilian embassy and had come solo to the party, though his host had heard she might be seeing someone at the Dutch embassy. No matter how subtly Ran camouflaged the inquiries about the woman, they all knew why he asked. Comments like "dangerous" and "dragon lady" from both men and women made her even more attractive to him.

When Cynthia finally glided out from the kitchen, Ran watched her from as far away as he could. Her skin color was coffee with just a spoonful of cream, making her golden brown. She wore a white sleeveless dress with tiny, blue glory-of-the-snow blossoms on it. He concluded that she was a stunningly beautiful woman.

Although petite, the timbre of her voice commanded attention and respect. She was like a firefly, her dress casting a bioluminescent light on the people she engaged while those close by hoped they would be next. She was playing the graceful hostess; she was the force in the room, and every-one knew it.

Ran waited his turn, approached her, and asked, "Can we meet somewhere tomorrow away from this crowd and talk with each other?"

"Yes," Cynthia said with a slight smile.

Whew, fantastic, yes!

"Tell me where?" he asked, pushing his luck.

He would drive to Timbuktu if he had to.

"I live in the Rainvill neighborhood," she replied with a warmer smile. "We could meet there at five after I finish work. It is twenty minutes from where you are staying."

She knows where I am staying? Ran thought, then said, "Tell me your address, I won't forget it."

Cynthia chuckled. "I'll have to warn my mother an American is coming to the house. You will understand when you meet her. The address is David Simonstrraat 81."

The following afternoon, Ran taxied early to David Simonstraat 81 and stepped around several road-killed snakes to get to Cynthia's house. He walked up the stairs where Cynthia's mother greeted him before he even knocked on the screen door. Alamelu was formally dressed for his visit and Ran observed the striking mother-daughter resemblance. The day before Cynthia had used the word *"warn,"* but her mother seemed ecstatic that he, an American, was in her house.

Alamelu told him Cynthia would be home soon and quickly made him feel at ease. She couldn't have been more welcoming and when he admired the giant avocados on the table, she jumped up, grabbed him by the hand, and took him out the back door and down the stairs to their avocado tree. They were as big as grapefruits. She picked three, then announced they would peel and enjoy them warm.

At that moment, Ran noticed something moving out of the corner of his eye. He turned and found himself eye to eye with a massive boa constrictor curled up in the Y of a tree trunk.

Alamelu laughed. "I am so sorry, I should have warned you. That is Elvis, the neighborhood boa. He's been around for years. Don't worry, he's never hungry because there are plenty of iguanas, rats, and stray dogs around for him to eat."

Ran walked backward toward the back steps, watching to see if Elvis moved. The huge snake seemed to be sleeping.

As he helped Alamelu prepare the avocados, he continued to look at Elvis through the window and marveled at what he saw.

A pest-control boa in the backyard, amazing!

Alamelu was in the middle of telling her family's history when Cynthia walked in. The two women switched to rapid-fire Dutch; he could tell the topic was tense and unpleasant. Cynthia helped herself to some avocado and wine, and then sat down across from him.

They laughed about his introduction to Elvis (he got points for not pissing his pants), and the women explained the difference between the vipers he stepped over on the street earlier and boas like Elvis. Drivers in the neighborhood would intentionally drive over the poisonous vipers that came from the canal alongside the street, but since the coup, the public works department had stopped working and the roadkill was left to rot on the street. With that, Alamelu made a graceful exit.

Alone, Ran said, "Thank you for allowing me to visit you in your home. I felt like we got off to a bad start for reasons we both know. I want to set the record straight between us before I leave tomorrow.

"The basketball coaches I met in Jamaica last December invited me here. I studied Suriname before I came. You know I am staying at Voss as a guest of the government. I met Bouterse there one time. I have loved working with sports people, but it is what I do. I have no respect for the military and their minions I met this week. Last night's party was a sweet time and made more so by experiencing you two days in a row. Now it is three."

He had asked Henke about Cynthia that morning, a mistake for sure. Henke had told him she was a known resistance member and was under surveillance. He shared that information with Cynthia and asked,

"Would you mind telling me about it?"

Cynthia went on to explain that Suriname had been Dutch Guyana until the Netherlands had granted it independence in 1975. The new government was unstable and General Desi Bouterse had staged a coup in 1980 and established a military government—with himself as the ruler. In 1982, fifteen journalists, educators, and lawyers who had opposed the military rule were taken from their beds to Fort Zeelandia, shot in the head, and gutted.

Cynthia had known all fifteen men; this was the circle in which she ran. One of the lawyers who had been killed was the husband of Cynthia's best friend, Jennifer. The night of the massacre, the wives had gone into hiding, afraid for their lives. Cynthia had had to identify Harold in a row on the floor at Fort Zeelandia.

Now eight months later, Jennifer had escaped to Holland and Cynthia was active in the underground resistance. She knew she was under heavy surveillance by the military and only trusted the few people in her immediate orbit.

As she concluded her story, Ran sat back on the couch and took a deep breath. He had heard parts of the story during the week, and now she had put all the pieces together. She had cried a bit as she had described entering Fort Zeelandia to identify Harold, but she ended the story seething with hatred for General Bouterse who ruled her country through fear, repression, and drug running.

At that moment, the setting sun sliced through the louvres of a window, spilling rays on them both. Ran would not have traded places with anyone on the planet at that moment; goose bumps arose on his arms and neck like an exclamation point to his thought.

"Thanks for sharing your story and trusting me. What can I do to help you?" he asked.

"Get our young players out of here so they can grow up strong and return to help us kick the asshole out," she answered with venom.

"Okay, a deal," Ran said. "I've identified six to eight players good enough to place and now I must find the schools that will accept them. The government's style depressed me this week, but to do it for you and your friends, that will motivate me to succeed."

Then he announced, "I've interrupted your life enough this evening, I'll go out and find a cab."

"I will take you back," she offered, standing up.

When they got in her car, she turned and looked squarely at Ran and said, "I want to be honest. The embassy community here was talking all week about how humble you were compared to the normal rude Americans. We don't like them as a rule. Full disclosure, I asked Stappie to invite me to his party so I could see for myself. I'm glad I did."

Ran about melted in his seat and for the second time that evening, goose bumps populated his arms and neck. That his emotions were so quick to surface on his body was new to him. He took another deep breath as she started the car.

In the Voss parking lot, Ran turned to her and said, "Can I stay in contact with you by letter and phone?"

"Yes," she replied quickly, "but you will have to send the letters to the embassy where I work because our home mail and phone are under surveillance."

"And your telephone number?" he asked, fingers crossed that she would agree to share her silky voice across the ocean.

"Yes, the same. It will be the Brazilian embassy's switchboard's number. My extension is seven," she answered.

She turned fully toward him, and when he did the same, she made the Thai gesture of thank-you, palms together across her chest with a bow of her head.

Then he curled his hands under hers, kissed her fingers gently, and some words spilled out of his mouth. This time she was the one who sat back and took a deep breath. He exited the car and walked up the steps to his room.

He had just made the last call for dinner at Voss, ordered some beans and rice a la carte, and tried to calm his emotions. The memory of kissing Cynthia's fingers and spontaneously telling her that he would rather be there with her than anywhere else in the world kept looping through his brain.

Ran had always been cautious and risk averse when he was around women with the potential for a relationship. But not the last hours with Cynthia. If a neutral observer had asked if there was a warm mutual attraction between them, Ran would have quickly answered, "Yes, absolutely!"

His body was a flashing neon sign that had to be unplugged soon or else.

The "or else" came quickly when Bouterse's advance men suddenly entered the dining room and ordered everyone to grab their food and leave. As Ran exited the door, the general was already waiting in the hallway, surrounded by armed bodyguards. He motioned for Ran to wait.

Fresh from Cynthia's gut-wrenching story and the possible romantic embers still smoldering, her hatred for the man standing in front of him was now his too. Ran watched

Bouterse closely as he finished a conversation with one of his soldiers. Ran thought of Napoleon and Mussolini, both short dictators, and was surprised that Bouterse, except for his military fatigues, looked like any other guy on the street.

"You are leaving early in the morning, right?" the general asked in a deferential tone.

"Yes, I've had an interesting week and thank you for supporting your basketball coaches," Ran answered, standing tall.

"Do you think you can get any of our good players a scholarship?" the general asked in a serious tone.

Ran responded, "I'm going to try."

"They tell me you like our women?" the general asked with a smile that men use when they begin to discuss this universal topic.

Ran stiffened but said, "Yes, of course! And the curry, too."

They locked eyes, mano a mano. Ran was four inches taller, forcing Bouterse to look up at him. The general turned and quickly entered the dining room without finishing their dialogue.

Ran walked out to the moonlit pool, stripped to his birthday suit, and dove into the deep end. He considered it his own private pool because no one else had used it all week. This would be his last peaceful swim.

Ten laps in as he glided underwater off the deep-end wall, he heard *crack crack* in his water-filled ears, and simultaneously two torpedo-like objects pierced the water in front of his head.

They were bullets, of course, which immediately lost their force in the water's drag and sank harmlessly to the four-meter bottom. Ran turned, treaded water, and looked up at Bouterse, who stood between two guards pointing their

guns at him. He was literally the sitting duck in the shooting gallery. Advantage Bouterse.

Now what, you little motherfucker? Ran thought, as he slowly paddled toward the shallow end, trying to catch his breath and slow his heart rate down.

"Stay away from the Bacchus girl. We know everything she and her Dutch-embassy boyfriend are planning. I am the president now. The sooner they are killed or leave Suriname, the better. Get some scholarships for our players, and you are always welcome here. Contact her again, and you are not."

With that threat, Bouterse and one guard returned to the main building. The other, holding his automatic, stood watch on the pool deck.

Attempting to flush the adrenaline out of his system, Ran swam ten more laps thinking he had had many lifeguards watch him swim, but none with a gun. He kept trying to connect his brain to his body, but he had to admit, fear was in the way.

From their conversation, Ran knew that Cynthia was aware that she was under surveillance. And now so was he, at least until the next morning.

After a sleepless night, mostly rattled by being shot at, but also thinking about being in Cynthia's house, a military vehicle picked him up, bypassed the airport check-in desk, and drove him directly to the airstair of the parked Suriname Airways plane.

Walking up the stairs, Ran turned to take one last look at his new-favorite country and spotted Cynthia sitting on the hood of her car parked behind the security fence. Surprised that she was there, he waved at her. She waved back.

Looking out the window as the airplane taxied for takeoff, he saw that she had slid off the hood and stood clutching the chain-link fence.

Wheels up and airborne, he closed his eyes, took a deep breath, and held it. *"Whew, my cup splashes over,"* he thought, *"the trajectories of Anisa, Cynthia, and Bouterse couldn't be more different, yet each has intersected my life."*

Exhaling slowly as the plane climbed through 10,000 feet, Ran had no idea how much one of them would influence the next chapters of his life.

Not Love

Ran's plate was full when he returned home from Suriname. He had to prepare his basketball team for its season and, at the same time, finish the divorce proceedings between himself and his wife of seventeen years. It was an uneven time for him.

Complicating his life even further, he had to deal with the image of the petite Hindu woman from Suriname that kept pinballing around inside his body until, to get some relief, he handwrote Cynthia a letter and sent it to the Brazilian embassy.

The short letter described how fascinated he had been listening to her story about the coup. He wanted to write, *"I find you attractive. Do you like me too? Maybe we could meet again?"* But he didn't.

Instead, his last paragraph was *"Meeting you and spending time in your home was the highlight of my summer. I'm hoping you'll find time to write back. Thanks."*

Without realizing it, he had taken the first *slow* step in the *slow, slow, quick quick, slow* of the ancient dance of love: the tango.

"There, I've done what I can do. Now I can forget about Cynthia and get on with my life," he foolishly told himself.

Driving back to Paramaribo the morning of his departure, Cynthia felt something new in the pit of her stomach. Until that moment, she had been immune to the romantic virus she had observed around her. She saw herself as being above all that drama, but she had to admit she was attracted to the American.

Driving, Cynthia asked her stomach, "Now what?"

Her stomach answered, "Something new, maybe a sweet discomfort?"

This new feeling made her laugh as she gripped the steering wheel tighter.

Plus, by the end of the day, she learned that Bouterse's men had shot at Ran while he was swimming in the pool. His warning to Ran about staying away from "the Bacchus girl" had surprised her underground comrades since no one was aware the two had met more than casually at the party.

When Cynthia got home, she had to put up with Alamelu, who was all over her about looking sick.

"Ha, finally lightning has struck," Alamelu said smugly. "I was starting to wonder if you would ever get the love light turned on. Where is he? Invite him to dinner tonight! I want to see you squirm."

"He flew home this morning," Cynthia answered. "I'll probably never see him again."

That night in the privacy of her room, she picked up the paper he had written his information on and, in a confusing moment, put it to her nose.

After a sleepless night, Cynthia pushed herself to get on with her work and resistance life. Like Ran, her plate was full, but now, surprisingly, there was room to daydream about what might happen if she ever saw the American again.

His letter arrived ten days later. She had been nonchalantly checking the daily mail pouch, hoping to see a personal letter with her name on it. Like a hungry dog spotting a bone, she grabbed the letter and ran to her office.

That night, Cynthia wrote him a two-page, single-spaced letter on yellow legal paper. She described the embassy community's sympathy for her name having come out of Bouterse's mouth and apologized for the danger she had put him in.

Her closing line was *"I loved receiving your letter and hope you'll find time to send me another. Take care."*

Cynthia never thought about why she included *"love"* in the closing, but it was her responding *slow* step to the ancient dance by teasing, *"Yes, I'm interested."*

So, their long-distance relationship began with Cynthia in the cocoon of the Brazilian embassy and Ran in the throes of his basketball season. They began to talk on the phone weekly, which had to take place when she was in her office. Of course, her colleagues rooted for her to have the American Bouterse had shot at for a boyfriend rather than the boring Dutch guy Cynthia spent time with.

They wrote about the details of their lives. Ran described life as a basketball coach and his waning interest in continuing it. Cynthia couldn't understand how coaching could be a paying job. He told her his age, forty, and that he had two children from a failed marriage. After working at universities for fifteen years, he was thinking about resigning and starting a company that arranged international trips for college teams.

Cynthia spoke Dutch, Spanish, Portuguese, English, and the Surinamese creole. Learning languages was easy for her and although just twenty-four, she was a sought-after talent at all the embassies in Paramaribo. Her nephew and niece lived with her and her mother. Her father had died ten years earlier, and she was the breadwinner for their house. The Dutch embassy was the underground center for the resistance against the dictator and she was managing the Hindu community's participation.

She was delighted to learn that Ran loved the popular movie *E.T.*, which was showing all over the world. Cynthia kidded that she was in love with E.T. Ran wished he was Elliott pedaling the flying bicycle.

Ran quit his coaching career at the end of the season to start his travel company. He thought there was a market to produce international trips for college teams. No such company existed in 1983.

He had experience in Antigua and Suriname and wanted to take a closer look at more Caribbean islands. So he planned a trip to St. Lucia, Saint Vincent and the Grenadines, Barbados, and Curacao. Tongue-in-cheek, he asked Cynthia to join him.

Cynthia said, "Yes, I would love to." She'd used that word again.

Ran told her he would get two rooms if that made her more comfortable. She had laughed. "No, let's stay in one, I don't bite."

As the departure day drew nearer, both became anxious about how it would go. Each knew it could be a disaster. But it wasn't a *blind date* they were embarking on; they had been communicating for nine months. Ran always asked how Elvis was doing and she wanted to know if his team won its last game.

She arrived at Vigie Airport in Castries, Saint Lucia, on Guyana Air and saw him standing on the tarmac through the plane's window. *"Okay, he's decent looking, for an American,"* she said, smiling and nodding her head.

Ran had arrived in Castries the day before Cynthia, checked into the Red Lion Hotel, and spent a restless night. His mind kept bouncing back and forth between the two uncertain things that were to begin the next day. Collecting information about each country's sport facilities would be easier than beginning a trip with a woman he barely knew. Cynthia scared him, and he second-guessed his decision to invite her.

But when he saw her walk down the airstair and wave at him, he knew he had made the right decision. Like at the Sunday night party in Paramaribo, he could hardly catch his breath as she approached him.

They hugged clumsily and then stumbled over each other. He caught her in his arms before she fell. It was an inauspicious moment for the two who had agreed to spend the next ten days together, but she seemed undaunted, and they laughed with each other as they headed toward the taxi.

For their first dinner, Ran had made a reservation at the Green Parrot Restaurant, at the time, the only five-star restaurant in the Caribbean. Edward "Chef Harry" Joseph met them at the door and immediately took to Cynthia, well, her beauty was what he took to. He fawned openly on her and gave them the best table in the house.

Reactions like Chef Harry's would be a recurring phenomenon wherever they went. Hotel maids, tennis court managers, government ministers, beachcombers, work gangs in trucks, you name it, they would snap to attention when they saw her. Then they would slowly stand down and acknowledge their good fortune, like they were seeing their first rainbow.

It was a distraction Cynthia was used to, but he was surprised at how uncomfortable it made him feel. As he watched the other restaurant guests' wide-eyed reactions to her, he realized he had no experience being with such a stunning woman.

How am I supposed to act? he asked himself.

Ran became acutely aware from the restaurant guests' stares that they questioned what the shining-star woman was doing with an average-looking man like Ran.

Ran wanted to stand up and yell at the full restaurant, "Goddamn it, I am not this woman's sugar daddy; she bought her own ticket here!"

But he didn't and decided to table the imbalance he felt in her presence until later. They would have plenty of time to discuss the topic as the same thing happened regularly throughout their days together.

With Chef Harry monitoring their table, they began their five-star experience.

Cynthia leaned over the table and quietly asked, "Are you really an American?"

"Why?" he asked, leaning in as well.

Almost whispering, she said, "You are eating two handed with the fork in your left hand." She continued waving the fork in her right hand, and said, "We can identify Americans by how they eat with one hand and push food around with their fingers. It's so gross, we call them American pigs."

He was delighted she had noticed how he ate. He had been taught the European style ten years earlier in Denmark when he was conducting basketball camps in Aarhus and now, like Cynthia, Ran would make fun of the way Americans ate.

It gave him an opening to make fun of himself, flamboyantly showing how he used to eat, then flashing his two-handed skills. She laughed out loud a lot and the whole scene made for a fine start to their trip. She took his hand as they left the Green Parrot.

They returned to their beach-level room at the Red Lion Hotel that opened to the sea, both feeling the awkwardness of what would happen next. Ran was determined to let the physical part of their relationship happen slowly and gently.

Likewise, Cynthia seemed to have no intention of jumping into bed with him the first hour. Privately, though, he wanted to make up for their fumbling embrace at the airport and he suspected she did too.

Taking his shoes off, he grabbed a beach towel.

"Let's pull those two beach chairs to the water and discuss the meaning of life," he said over the crashing waves.

The moon was in its waxing gibbous phase, heading toward full, and the sky was clear, so there was plenty of light shining on them and the water.

Both were exhausted from their long flights and the uncertainty cloud that hung over their decision to spend time together in one hotel room. Who would make the first move?

They were quietly absorbing the sounds of the sea and the moonlight when Cynthia stood up, took off her clothes, and walked into the water. Her gleaming golden-brown skin reflected the moonlight as she slid into the water.

"Is there a dream dreaming me?" Ran wondered as he watched her.

"The water is cold! Would you hold me?" she yelled.

"Let me think about that." He laughed. He undressed quickly and waded into the water.

They had just embraced in chest-high water when a surprise wave rolled them upside down. He held her as they spun; they came up sputtering and laughing. Facing him, she jumped up to straddle his hips and gave him a saltwater kiss. He feigned fainting back into the water and they came up with mouthfuls of salty kisses. And laughs.

Back in their chairs, he dried her quickly and covered her with his towel. The night was warm, and they began to talk about the next day when she became silent. She had fallen asleep.

Ran sat on the edge of his chair, looked at her in the moonlight, and whispered, "Hmm, yep, no wonder General Bouterse wants to kick you out of Suriname. You are gorgeous, you have that great voice and enough elan vital to fill this Caribbean Sea."

He let her sleep for a while, retrieved their clothes from the sand, and then picked her up and carried her to the queen bed in their room. He lit a small candle, checked that she was covered well, and slipped in beside her. He fell asleep listening to her breathe.

They did not make love the next morning and showered separately.

The next night as they were walking barefoot on the beach, he stopped in front of her, put his arms around her, and kissed her softly. They stood in knee-deep water and held each other for minutes, this time without stumbling.

When they returned to the room, she shed her clothes and slid under the covers. He brushed the sand off his feet, quickly used the bathroom, and returned to another episode of sleeping beauty.

Cynthia could fall asleep quickly, in any position, and immediately go into a deep sleep where nothing could wake her. It was Ran's first experience with someone who could fall asleep instantly and he wondered if it was her strategy to avoid having sex with him.

On their third day, once done with the meetings and at lunch with the minister of sport, Cynthia called Ran out, pretending to show him a Saint Lucian painting, and asked, "Ran, would you make love to me this afternoon?"

"Let me think about it," he said and gestured, looking up at the painting, head cocked with his finger on his chin.

The two previously tentative people returned to their room and the dam broke. They woke up the next morning in each other's arms and smiling at the ceiling.

Cynthia was not a virgin. She had had casual sex before and afterward had asked herself, "That's it? What's all the fuss about?"

That morning, she remembered Alamelu's comment about lightning striking her; maybe it had caused the heat Cynthia felt with Ran. "That's it!" she said with a smile. It was a sentence.

He had planned his island itinerary to see if island sport facilities were good enough to use for his new business. The idea of inviting Cynthia had bubbled up in the middle of his plans and after the first three days in Castries, they couldn't keep their hands off each other.

The next morning they boarded a Liat plane and headed to Saint Vincent and the Grenadines.

After Castries, Cynthia understood Ran's mission with the island sports people. That Cynthia became the lead negotiator in their meetings was his good fortune. Already a veteran of many synthetic embassy parties, she had learned the proper protocol and banter required. Ran was the novice with good intentions but awkward manners.

She demanded they enter the offices as cool professionals, that is, she was his lowly, note-taking assistant and he was the humble American asking questions. They were to give no clues of the intimate joy they had begun to share.

So the two of them would enter a government sport office, the ministers would stare at her, and she would quietly take a notepad out of her briefcase and look down. Ran, having a hard time not laughing out loud, would take a deep breath and let everyone in the room catch theirs.

With his best poker face, he would introduce "Miss Bacchus" as his "road secretary" and get right down to business. The island men and women at the table knew, the two lovers knew they knew, but they kept the ruse on as they walked out the door. Oh, they had great fun.

Ran's biggest problems were that he talked too much and too quickly.

For example, when one Vincentian official described how they had suspended their women's league for two years to "eliminate lesbians," he practically yelled, "You can't do that. It won't work. Lesbians are the best players all over the world!"

Cynthia had kicked his shin hard under the table and scolded him severely afterward.

"Look, I know attitudes are changing," she said, "but not in the islands or other Black cultures, not yet. Did they ask you what you believe?"

"No," he apologized.

"Then be quiet."

Sixteen years her senior, Ran had ridden many emotional roller coasters with only a large reserve tank of curiosity to keep him moving along. He had no natural gifts or talents, only that he could persevere and preferred to be lost scratching his way forward rather than sinking in quicksand. Plus, he could learn new things, including how to keep his mouth shut.

After the morning meeting and lunch with the minister of sport in Kingstown's centrum, they escaped down the road to the beach at Johnson Point.

There, in the late afternoon, two younger men came to their area of the beach and went back into a small hidden area and pulled out their sailboards. Curious about the odd couple on their beach, they stopped to interrogate the two.

Once satisfied that the foreigners were not dangerous, the two men jumped on the sailboards for their commute home to Bequia, the nearest of the Grenadines, nine miles away. They would return to their jobs in Kingstown the next morning on the same wind.

Sitting facing south on the beach with the sun setting to the west, Ran and Cynthia watched the two men get smaller and smaller and then poof! They were gone.

Neither had seen anything like that before and Cynthia laughed. "No traffic today, they'll get home quickly."

The moment had a profound effect on both.

Throughout the years of their long-distance discussions, one would ask, "Where are you?" and the other would answer, "Bequia."

Or one would ask, "What are you doing?" and the other would reply, "Going to Bequia."

Their sighs would take them back immediately to the awe they had felt the moment the boards had disappeared that day.

When away from doing his business, their discussions while walking the beaches were like two playground kids on a seesaw. Imagine Ran, eighty pounds heavier, holding his end down with her up high, would listen to her as she talked down to him about why America was perceived as the heavy-handed imperialist of the world.

"Huh, really?" he said, looking up at her.

"The arrogance of Ronald Reagan and the hubris of your aggressive capitalism make all of us small people and countries hate you," she hissed at him. "Do you understand Ran?"

"I do," he replied. "You used the word 'hubris.' What exactly does that mean?" he asked.

"We have been using that word in our embassy lately," she answered. "In Portuguese it is *arrogancia*."

"Okay, I get it," he acknowledged from the bottom. It was an aha moment for Ran and the first time he had heard such a blunt opinion of *his* country.

There were the give-and-take discussions when they balanced at midpoint on the board, and he had to scoot up from his end to weigh less. Topics like religion, race, why white people can't dance, and Anisa, the Kenyan woman he had escorted to the market, were all discussed openly with their four feet dangling off the ground while they were looking into each other's eyes.

Ran had told Cynthia about his experience with Anisa and what she had told him that Saturday morning.

Cynthia asked, "Do you think she would ever change her trajectory to a completely different life?"

"I don't know, but I would guess not," he answered.

"I agree, because we have been trying to get the Brazilian prostitutes who work in Paramaribo to change. The embassy gives them money and other incentives, but so far, no success. It drives me crazy."

They exchanged opinions and beliefs freely and without judgment; no topics were off-limits. They required a sense of humor. Fortunately, each had a healthy one.

One of the lingering questions from their balanced teeter-totter board was "*What happens to you when you die?*" came up again on their short flight from St. Vincent to Barbados.

Cynthia's mother was Hindu, and her father was Muslim. They had sent her to the Netherlands Catholic School, not only because it was the highest-ranked school in Paramaribo, but to add to her general education.

Her parents viewed religion as a subject, like geography and history, nothing more. Cynthia thought their sending her to the Catholic school was proof of their sense of humor.

Ran had not been so fortunate. Instead, the random card he drew was an evangelical Baptist church in a small rural village. Fire and brimstone were featured in every message, and depending how obedient one was to the jealous god, he either ended up with eternal life in heaven or burning painfully in hell.

A sense of humor and laughing were considered tools of the devil.

"Wait, did you believe all this?" she asked.

"From the beginning, I considered myself genetically impaired to believe but had to pretend I was one of them to get along. We knew nothing about the world outside of our county line."

Cynthia was fascinated to know a person who had been exposed to such imaginary rules. She kept peppering him with questions about his religious history as they walked into the Hilton Barbados.

Ran stopped and asked her, "If you would not be too embarrassed, I, a white American man, invite you, a golden-brown Hindu woman, to attend a Baptist Church with me tomorrow morning. Think of it as going on a glass-bottom boat excursion where we can see all the fish below," he finished with a big smile.

It was Saturday and he knew there had to be a Baptist Church in Bridgetown. At check-in, Ran asked the front desk clerk and as luck would have it, the clerk was a member of the Emmanuel Baptist Church.

"Ha, we are going to church tomorrow and get your soul saved," Ran declared with a smile.

She giggled as only she could.

"You've been sinning a lot these days," he added, wagging his finger at her, "and this will be an opportunity to ask for forgiveness. To wipe the slate clean, if you will."

"Forgive me for what?" she said, wagging her finger back at him. "I have never felt so alive. I'm not changing anything! Isn't this heaven?"

They hugged each other tightly.

The two walked hand in hand to church that Sunday morning. Strange attendees they were, as she was the only brown person and he the only white person. The congregation was all Black. She took her folding hand-fan to minimize sweating and he knew the words to most of the sad songs.

In the normal island church competition to be the most beautiful woman at the service, Cynthia won easily and without a colorful Sunday bonnet of the kind worn by all the Bajan women. They were warmly welcomed afterward with many of the women just wanting to touch the shining, golden-brown woman.

"Thank you for taking me to church, Ran. Another first with you. For sure the mystery of what happens when you die is a wonderful question. I read something recently about an Egyptian myth that I want to try on you."

"I'm all ears, my dear."

They had been walking through Queen's Park and sat down under the giant baobab tree.

Cynthia began, "The myth is that you can only get into the hereafter (the Baptist heaven) if your heart is lighter than a feather. So unlike your stories of cowering under a mad god, our assignment here is to work on keeping a light heart."

"We are talking about keeping a healthy sense of humor and being able to laugh at oneself, right?" he asked.

"Yes, it seems so, and no matter how bad a situation is, one has to find a laugh somehow, like we have been doing," she added.

"A feather, huh? From what kind of bird?" he asked.

"Ha, there you go being a white guy again. It doesn't matter, Ran!" she yelled.

Bowing his head in deference to her, he replied, "Good point. Count me in. It is a beautiful myth."

Up early the next morning, feather on his mind, and enthused about the Egyptian road to the hereafter, Ran looked for a local tattoo parlor. He was told there was such an artist who worked in a small room at the Boatyard Club just ten minutes from the Hilton. He found "Old Sammie" reading the local paper with his feet on the table.

He made two appointments starting at 1 p.m. that afternoon. It was their last day in Barbados, and he returned to the hotel to tell her about his idea.

"A feather tattoo? Where?" she asked.

He pointed. "On that perfect ass of yours, of course."

"My mother will kill me!" she exclaimed.

"Tell her I made you do it," he replied and added, "if I read the tea leaves correctly, she's on my side."

With a shake of her head, Cynthia admitted, "I would not be here with you if she had not pushed me."

As they walked to the Boatyard, they agreed their feathers had to be different, that the choice would be private, and that each would not look at the other's until they returned to the hotel and dropped their pants together in front of the floor-length mirror.

Cynthia went first. Hers took over an hour as Sammie took his sweet time tattooing her golden ass. She took Ran's place on the dock. His tattoo took thirty minutes, and they returned to the hotel, holding hands all the way.

In front of a mirror with a sea breeze blowing through a window, they dropped their pants and took turns admiring each other's feather. Then, sitting on the floor and avoiding touching their tattoos, they made love as they often had by stroking each other with their fingertips. She climaxed first and immediately fell asleep in his arms. At dinner, they celebrated their new religion as they prepared to travel to Curacao, their last stop.

They had laughed at and with each other from that first night in St. Lucia, adopted a new mythology, branded themselves with a feather, and suddenly found themselves at the end of their trip. They had begun to like each other more and touch fingers like E.T. and Elliott, but neither wanted to "go home."

Home for Cynthia was a mystery. The government could have tracked her to St. Lucia on the one-way ticket she had bought in Paramaribo, but not the one she had returned on from Curacao. She wasn't the ringleader in the anti-government movement, just a lowly lieutenant working under the cover of the embassy.

She was right, they weren't paying attention. *This time.*

Like Suriname, Curacao was a former Dutch colony but without the storm cloud of a military coup raining over it. They stayed in the Grand Villa V-07, the grandest VIP house at the Las Palmas Resort in Willemstad. Just like their first night at the Green Parrot, they got the usual "beautiful woman" upgrade. Ran never stopped musing at this phenom-enon, but he had adjusted to it during the past ten days.

It was in Curacao where they invented an intimate game with fresh mangos and passion fruits, both abundant on the island. They had discovered that passion fruit was Ran's favorite fruit and mango was Cynthia's.

But after deep discussion between the two lovers and the microscopic evaluation of their souls, Cynthia became his passion fruit because of her fierce, crunchy, and tart person-ality. Ran became her favorite mango, sweet, juicy, and with strings between his teeth.

They would peel the mango, cut the passion fruit open, and eat sweet and sour together. No water, no towel, no clothes . . . just tongues, mouths, noses, skin, fingers, and hands.

They would suck the mango seed clean and leave some passion seeds on each other for later detection and consump-tion. It was a long and sensuous game and, in their light-hearted opinions, gave them a leg up on Hel and Hana, the stage-four lovers in Trevanian's *Shibumi*.

Done with his official meetings, he wanted to contact Anisa if he could find her. When she had left Ran at the market in Suriname, she told him she was coming to Curacao. The two had talked about Anisa often and both were frustrated they couldn't change Anisa's kind of life. Cynthia was eager to meet this woman who had impacted Ran so powerfully.

They drove out to Campo Alegre, the government-run brothel, and asked for her. Soon, Anisa, not Lula, came out to greet them. She took them up to the dining area where other women were eating.

Anisa was okay. Yes, the stress was less, but the clientele was mostly seamen, which Ran knew was not a good thing in her line of work. Since the brothel was run and regulated by the government, she made more money and felt safer.

She knew immediately that Cynthia was Surinamese and asked if there had been any changes in the government. The couple shared small details of their journey to Curacao. Each person at the table was sensitive to the different trajectories their lives were on, yet all three felt equal. Ran and Cynthia gave her their phone numbers and addresses just in case they could ever help her.

When they were leaving, Anisa asked them, in her natural, earthy voice, "How are you two going to make your love stay?"

The two stopped in their tracks, looked at each other with tilted heads, and rolled their eyes.

They had avoided that universal term *"love"* on purpose and preferred their phrase *"I would rather be here now with you than anywhere else in the world."* Each had enjoyed spending time with the other. Neither had any desire to control the other.

As they were driving back to the Las Palmas, Cynthia turned to Ran and asked, "Are we in love?"

"Hmm, I wonder," he responded. "It seems to me that we should at least discuss the answer to Anisa's question. It might take a lifetime."

They agreed to table this discussion until their final night and to have it on the floating bridge in Willemstad at sunset.

That same night, Cynthia woke him at 2 a.m. and said, "I challenge you to a one-set match. The winner gets to give the loser a two-hour massage."

It was where they were in their relationship at that moment, since both found more joy in giving than receiving.

"Uhh one condition," she said, laughing at him. "We are playing in the nude."

"Ha, you think watching your naked body glide around the court will distract my superior skill? No chance, my dear, let's go." He patted her ass with his tennis racket.

So, at 2:15 a.m., a small brown woman and a tall white man walked down the hill to the tennis court, each with a tennis racket and a towel. The court lights were on all night, and they hoped the night watchman would find their escapade funny.

She was serious and wanted to win badly; after all, it was her idea. He would go on to play tennis on all the continents of the world, but this match would be his lifetime favorite. With the score 5-5, she hit two amazing, first-time-ever shots to win the set. Ran was delighted for her.

The two sweaty humans sat on their towels and laughed at themselves. He helped her up, gave her his racket, and picked her up like he had the first night in St. Lucia. They began to lick the salty sweat off each other on the way back to the villa and finished that fun in their bed.

They had postponed, until that final night, the dreaded discussion about love, their future, and all the gooey questions that bubble up between humans who more than like each other.

An hour before sunset, they headed to the floating bridge that connected the Punda and Otrobanda quarters of Willemstad. Known as the Swinging Lady by the locals, the Queen Emma Bridge by the Dutch who built it, its 548-foot length floated on sixteen pontoons. It served as a busy walking bridge between the two quarters and when required, the "Lady" would swing to the Otrobanda side to allow ocean vessels to enter the Saint Anna Bay.

Because of its construction and the sea, the Lady was always moaning and groaning. During those three days in Curacao, they had often leaned on the rails and just listened.

Cynthia leaned on the west rail and Ran held her from behind.

His chin on her shoulder, he said, "She sounds like us, the subtle crackling energy we have together. What is she saying?"

Cynthia replied, "I want you, I need you, I have to have you!" Silence. "Ha, I'm just kidding!"

He held her tighter.

"Do I love you, Ran?"

"You don't have to."

"Do I love you, Cynthia?"

"You don't have to."

Silence.

"Damn," he swore, "listening to the Old Lady sighing on our last night is too sad. Let's go get dinner." He reached for her hand.

They walked to the restaurant at the Otrobanda Hotel, where Ran had reserved a balcony table overlooking the channel and the bridge. It was dusk, the Lady was lit, and the lights from Punda side were clicking on one by one. They stared at the gorgeous view and slowly turned to each other.

Cynthia was laughing at herself crying. "I've never lived so freely and now I'm returning to my other life. I am missing us already and it makes me cry? What am I supposed to do now?" she pleaded.

Great question. What were these two going to do now after ten days of zigzagging across the southern Caribbean? Both acknowledged the odds of them being this compatible and enjoying each other had been slim at best.

Cynthia was younger than Ran but more mature in most things. She had seen fifteen men she knew with holes in the head and gutted. She was an important person in the Suriname resistance and under constant surveillance. She was stunningly beautiful and understood the superficiality of the false currency it gave her. She didn't like Americans, but now there was one sitting in front of her whom she more than liked.

Starting a new chapter in his life, Ran was trying to blow wind in the sail of his new tour business. Lacking financial capital, he was aware that any success would require a twenty-four-seven commitment. He embraced uncertainty and the inconsistencies of human behavior. His brain was wide open and nothing humans did shocked him. He was aware that relationships without mystery bored him.

And there they were that night, two independent human beings who had never wanted to rely on anyone, slobbering all over the other as if their lives would end tomorrow.

Naturally they talked about the sexual intimacy they shared, how it started slowly and then exploded. There was lots of laughing and sighs. By dessert they had returned to the love question.

Ran started, "I'm not sure what love is or means, but I know these days with you will age sacred in me. I will more than miss you. To say I love you seems too cheap."

Cynthia chimed in, "I would rather be with you here now than anywhere else in the world, Ran. Is this love?"

"Could be. I prefer all those words over love. Perhaps this is who we are my dear, a rendezvous and then separation back to our regular lives."

"Yes, maybe," she replied, leaving *"maybe"* hanging on the line.

"By the way, you could be pregnant, Cynthia."

"I am not supposed to be able according to my doctor, but if I am, well, my mother would be happy. I'm not sure about me. How would you feel?" she asked him straightaway.

"I am not sure either, Cynthia," Ran answered seriously, "but he or she would be a striking human being, don't you think?"

His question floated toward the sunset.

Hand in hand, they returned to the Lady.

"We keep bringing up 'missing you,' which seems as inadequate as the shortcut 'love,'" Ran noted.

"I agree." She continued. "Missing seems to be less than how I am feeling. I think my heart is going to explode. Could we use the word 'yearning' instead? Remember how E.T.'s heart would glow red surrounded by a blue aura? It seems warmer and softer and more like us."

Venice has its Bridge of Sighs and that evening the two christened the Swinging Lady as their *Bridge of Yearning*. It would be a sacred place they would return to throughout their lives, sometimes together and sometimes alone. Either way, their hearts would glow like E.T.'s and bring tears to their eyes.

The next morning, Cynthia flew south and Ran flew north. And the yearning began. Something else, too.

Panita

Cynthia found herself barely holding on to a runaway train when she returned home from Curacao. She yearned for Ran every minute of every day. Bouterse's men had visited the Brazilian embassy and asked questions about her absence, which were answered in a protective way. Her colleagues knew where she went and were fighting against the Bouterse government, so covering for her was natural.

When Cynthia returned to the Dutch embassy, Eric, her close friend who worked for the Dutch foreign service, declared his love for her and asked her to take a more active role in the resistance. When she stirred Eric's two requests with her yearning for Ran, she found herself tied up in knots.

About to jump off the train, she missed her period and started feeling, well, pregnant.

A gynecological assessment a year earlier had suggested she could not get pregnant, which is why she had brushed off Ran's question in Curacao. However, after missing her second period, she and Alamelu visited the gynecologist to confirm.

The grandmother-to-be was thrilled.

The mother-to-be was not.

Cynthia's pregnancy was a private event. Her mother, sister, and two aunts knew Ran was the father. All took a vow of secrecy to protect Cynthia and everyone at David

Simonstraat 81. Bouterse's government had been identifying her resistance friends and sending them out of the country randomly.

She hid her body's changes well and carried her baby to full term without anyone else knowing except her gynecologist. Of course, her Brazilian colleagues were suspicious but kept their lips sealed for her safety.

She was painfully conflicted about whether to tell Ran or not. She feared he would immediately come to Suriname and risk his and her lives. The local government's punitive restraints on its citizens, the new hormones rushing around in her body, and the thick yearning she felt for Ran made each day a challenge.

Finally, Panita, glorious, beautiful girl in Hindi, was born January 21, 1985, exactly nine months and ten days after the two lovers left Curacao. Although she put Ran's name on Panita's birth certificate at the Academic Hospital in Paramaribo Cynthia, she never told Ran she was pregnant.

Ran wouldn't find out about Panita until twelve years later.

Four weeks after giving birth and suffering from postpartum depression, Cynthia and ten others were declared persona non grata by the government. She was given seven days to leave Suriname. She finally let go of the runaway train's window rail and tumbled to Costa Rica with Eric, her soon-to-be-husband.

She left her blue-eyed baby at home with Alamelu.

It was a natural handover for Panita's grandmother to take responsibility for her daughter's baby and Mamalu, grandmother in Hindi, was ecstatic with her sacred assignment.

Cynthia was a wreck when she arrived in Costa Rica. She was surprised at how much she missed holding Panita and yearned for Ran to the point of being sick at times. To complicate her life even more, Eric kept professing his love for her and wanted to know why she wouldn't love him back.

"He will never understand," she would say to the ceiling in her bed in her private room at the official residence of the Dutch foreign service.

Cynthia knew her mother would be a solid rock on which Panita would grow; the girl would not be one of those children thrown around among their warring families. At the time, Cynthia was at peace with her decisions to keep Panita in Suriname and not tell Ran. Over time, however, this decision would begin to weigh on her heavily.

Eric knew about Ran, and, of course, Panita. He had made it abundantly clear he didn't want any part of raising another man's daughter. Alamelu wouldn't have let him have her anyway.

To Cynthia, her relationship with Eric was a business arrangement—both got something they wanted. She offered the Dutch diplomat a beautiful escort and skilled host for the official embassy parties. Standing beside Eric in the official greeting lines, she enabled him to look more impressive and climb the ranks faster.

As her part of the bargain, she would receive 50 percent of all assets accrued by the couple and come and go as she pleased. She was never required to answer to Eric about her whereabouts.

It took fourteen months after Cynthia and Ran had left Curacao before she felt healthy enough to invite him to Costa Rica. Although they wrote to each other and talked on the phone, he had almost given up hope that he would see her again.

Ran accepted that the turmoil she had been through in

moving to Costa Rica was the reason why they couldn't meet sooner. He was never suspicious of the secret she was hiding.

Cynthia picked up Ran at the Juan Santamaria International Airport and headed for the Cloud Forest near the Arenal Volcano. They were like two caged animals let loose for the first time. They made mad, passionate love on and off for twenty-four hours before they relaxed and talked. They ended their time together in the Limon area on the north beaches of Costa Rica and held each other while they watched the monkeys return to their roosts in the trees at dusk.

In those first years of Panita's life, the elephant in the room was Cynthia's inability to predict how Ran would react to finding out Panita existed. She was unwilling to gamble telling him the truth for fear of losing her time with him.

During the next eleven years, they met in Costa Rica again, Michigan, Wisconsin, Puerto Rico, the Bahamas, Australia, back to Curacao, Cuba, and the Netherlands. Always desperate to hold her, Ran would go wherever she chose and carried his sleeping beauty to bed all over the globe.

Always urgently needing to fill her empty tank, Cynthia never told him, and her guilt kept piling up.

Her diplomatic life had become that of a concubine, looking pretty and proper at government parties and sharing an icy bed with the second-in-command. She hosted too many cocktail parties and was forced to listen to the bleached conversations of proper women. Smiling at them and pitying them at the same time, Cynthia knew none had ever had warm mango juice licked from their breasts, let alone a passion fruit seed nibbled off the morning after.

Cynthia and Ran's rendezvous were dependent on her foreign-service post locations and the constant changes didn't bother Ran. He never asked for more.

In fact, he felt more than lucky to spend time with Cynthia, who, nine years into their relationship, had gained a high-level rank in the Dutch foreign service. Their physical relationship had remained robust and their postcoital bliss conversations were medicine for both.

Back in Paramaribo, Panita was five years old when it dawned on her that the mysterious woman, Cynthia, who brought her presents from time to time, was her real mother. Until that moment, Mamalu had been her mother and life was idyllic on Simonstraat 81. Panita had her aunts, uncles, and cousins to love her.

So, Panita had a grandmother and now formally a mata, mother in Hindi. She began calling Cynthia mata; it was a bit awkward at first, but Panita enjoyed having a mother like all the rest of the kids.

From the first day she entered Saint Louise School, blue-eyed, light-skinned Panita proved to be a force that the nuns had to deal with daily, both good and scary. Panita was taller and ran faster than the boys. Her innate confidence, along with a low aptitude for obedience, kept her in constant trouble. Secretly, though, the nuns called her Super Girl and loved teaching their brightest student.

Panita never lacked self-confidence until, walking home from school, her best friend, Asti, asked her, "Who is your father?"

Eleven-year-old Panita stopped.

"I don't know, should I know?" she asked.

No one had ever asked her, and she had never asked herself.

"Do you know, Asti?"

"No, but I have heard other people asking each other," Asti confessed.

"So really, I have a father?" Panita asked with some exasperation.

"Yes, I think they are required," Asti declared.

Panita ran the rest of the way home and asked Mamalu, "Who is my father?"

It was the first time the grandmother hesitated to respond to the granddaughter.

Steadying her voice, she said, "Oh, my *carino*, let's ask your mother when she comes next time. It is time for you to know. She's coming home soon."

Panita went to the back steps at Simonstraat 81 and started to count her friends' fathers. She was shocked that they all had one. Okay, some were in the house, some not, and some divorced. She had a basic understanding of what divorce meant.

Until that day, Panita's world had been neat and clean; she was an innocent girl. Her brain's shelves were perfectly arranged in straight lines. She was living a carefree and happy life in Paramaribo.

But Asti's question smashed that perfect world into pieces. Like all her friends, she had to have one, but *Who was he? Where was he? Was there something wrong with her? Was it her fault he wasn't there?*

She was confused and sad for the first time and would remember that uncomfortable moment for the rest of her life.

"Really, why the big secret?" she asked Elvis out loud.

Panita walked back into the house and dialed Cynthia's number in Den Haag. The housekeeper answered and took Panita's message. "Call me. It's urgent!"

After Panita had fallen asleep that night, Alamelu called Cynthia and told her that Panita had asked the question.

Since Panita's birth, mother, daughter, and the whole family had agreed that Cynthia would be the one to tell Panita when the time came.

Cynthia booked a flight for two days later. Now traveling on a Dutch diplomatic passport, she could enter Suriname without fear of reprisal from Bouterse. She went to bed that night and talked to the ceiling, as she often did. "Panita, my love, you are in for a big surprise."

News spread in the family about why Cynthia was suddenly coming home, and all agreed it was time. Naturally, Panita considered Cynthia her mother, but her mother was less important to her than Mamalu. She thought it must be a big secret if Mamalu wouldn't tell her.

She didn't understand what Cynthia did for a living or why she didn't live with them. She knew Cynthia had a husband and wondered, *Is Eric my father?* Whatever the case, Panita just wanted to be like the rest of her friends and at least have a father to claim.

Cynthia's flight arrived in the morning. Panita came home from school to the living room where Cynthia and Ran had first talked. No one else was allowed in the house. When Panita returned home, she sat down across from Cynthia.

"I want to tell you about the first time I met your father and the days we spent together that made you," she began. She went on to tell Panita the short, G-rated version of their time together. When she finished, Cynthia began to weep.

Panita was startled. She had never seen her mother show any emotion.

"Wait, he's not Dutch? He's an American?" Panita asked, sitting up straighter.

Cynthia wiped her eyes with the back of hands and said, "Yes."

"Do you have a picture of him?" Panita, asked, not containing the excitement in her voice.

Cynthia reached into her purse and held out a photo. "This one is from last month when we were together at my apartment in Den Haag."

Panita sat back and looked at her father, amazed to be seeing her parents together for the first time. Then without warning, photo still in her hand, she jumped up, bolted out the door, and sprinted to Asti's house, usually fifteen minutes away, this time ten. Asti knew this was the day and what her out-of-breath friend was about to share.

They went out to Asti's screened porch and Panita ordered, "Sit down."

She stood in front of her friend and proudly displayed the picture. "Ta da. Here is my father! He's an A-mer-i-can!"

Asti was surprised. The rest of the Hindu community would be surprised too; everyone assumed Panita's father was Dutch. For sure, it was less than desirable for a Hindu to mix genes with a Dutch. But an American, well, that was something. Light the fireworks. Start the celebration!

Panita sat down next to Asti, and they passed the photo back and forth.

"What's his name?" Asti asked.

"Ran," Panita answered.

"His last name? It can be yours, too, I think," Asti pressed.

"Uh, she didn't tell me." Panita jumped up. "Bye!"

"Goodbye Miss America, my best friend!" Asti declared with pride and placed her hand across her heart.

The girls hugged and giggled, and Panita ran home.

Cynthia's visits home were usually tense. Her quick, confrontational temper always disrupted the family's easy rhythm as she had no patience with the petty arguments they wanted to have. She could hold grudges and did so against various members, sometimes for years.

Everyone generally knew she lived a double life, but she never shared any details. They knew she owned apartments in Amsterdam's centrum and Den Haag. She flew first class on Suriname Airways and KLM and used her diplomatic passport to skip lines. Those were details she did share.

When Panita returned home from Asti's, the house was abnormally quiet. Cynthia was in Alamelu's bedroom; they were lying together and talking quietly. Panita joined them, wiggled in between and listened to Cynthia talk about when she met Ran and how he met Elvis when he came to their house the first time.

Cynthia explained that Ran had come along before she had married Eric. She emphasized that Ran was still her special friend.

Continuing, Cynthia told Panita that Ran did not know that he had a daughter in Suriname. She apologized to Panita for not telling Ran, but it flew right over Panita's head given all the new information she was processing. Cynthia cried softly during her confession while Alamelu held her.

Later, the three of them had a quiet dinner. Aunts, uncles, and cousins meandered in and out, all seeking private time with Cynthia. Warm hugs were shared, and genuine happiness reigned at Simonstraat 81 that night.

The next morning, Cynthia gave Panita a copy of her birth certificate with Ran's name listed as father along with an envelope full of pictures of the two of them together in different countries.

Mother and daughter laid all the photos on the dining room table and Cynthia told Panita where they were taken and when. They had so much fun with Panita ranking her parents standing on the top of the Arenal Volcano in Costa Rica and in front of the Riviera Hotel in Havana as her two favorites.

Having gotten off the previous night's emotional roller coaster, Cynthia told Panita, "I'm going to tell your father about you in two months when we meet in Amsterdam. He will melt when he sees your pictures. I know him well. Then he will call you."

Listening to this news, Panita began to look forward to hearing her father's voice. *And then what*, she wondered.

The departure morning Cynthia came to Panita's bedroom wearing only a night shirt and panties. She held something in her hand that she placed on the dresser. "There's something I want to show you," she said. Cynthia pulled her pants down and showed her feather tattoo on her right hip cheek.

"Wow!" Panita shouted, "Can I touch it?"

Cynthia nodded, and Panita traced the outlines with her finger.

"Your father has one too," Cynthia told her with a sly smile. "We got them in Barbados the day you were conceived, at least it is my fantasy. Wait, do you know what conceived means?"

"No." Panita shrugged, and Cynthia didn't bother to explain.

"His tattoo is different from mine," Cynthia said, "but it's a feather too."

"There's more to that story, and perhaps we will share it with you at some point. And I want to give this to you." She picked up the item on the dresser and handed it to Panita. "Please hold on to this for the three of us."

It was a VHS of *E.T.*, an older movie Panita had heard about but had never seen. She looked at Cynthia with her *why* face.

"Your father and I both love it," was Cynthia's answer.

Panita walked her mother to the taxi, and they shared warm, meaningful hugs for the first time. This was a breakthrough visit for mother and daughter.

For the first time in her life, Panita said, "Goodbye, Mata, I love you." And she meant it.

Cynthia's KLM flight home to Amsterdam was smooth, but the severe thunderstorms and turbulence in her body caused her to vomit twice at thirty-seven thousand feet to the point at which a flight attendant informed the pilot they had a very sick passenger on board.

She wasn't surprised by how well it went when she told Panita about Ran. But sitting in her first-class seat, looking into her makeup mirror, she saw a selfish woman looking back at her. She had second-guessed her assumption from the beginning that Ran would have insisted on taking Panita to the United States when he learned about her. She knew him better now and believed he would have agreed that Panita should grow up in Suriname.

Cynthia knew that Ran would not have eagerly rendezvoused with her all over the world if he had known of Panita. On this charge, she pleaded guilty to desperately needing those times for her soul more than telling him the truth. The selfish guilt she acknowledged turned her stomach upside down and made her heart heavier than the 747 she was flying on.

Two months later, Ran arrived in Amsterdam three days earlier than the basketball team he would escort through Europe. Like always, Cynthia was to pick him up at Schiphol Airport and they planned to hold each other for three days straight. But she called him before he departed and told him she couldn't pick him up and asked him to meet her at the Garoeda Restaurant for dinner. This should have been Ran's first clue that things were about to change.

He caught the train to town, checked into the Golden Tulip Riverside Hotel, their favorite, and that evening headed to the Garoeda Restaurant in Amsterdam's centrum.

Their dinner hadn't gone well. Cynthia was not her normal, lighthearted self. First, she told him she couldn't stay the night as she was under heavy surveillance by her husband.

Eric had finally gotten tired of her long-term affair with Ran and had asked for a divorce. Cynthia's high-priced Dutch attorney had advised her to stop the pleasure trips or risk losing her painfully earned property in the Dutch court. Ran could sense that Cynthia was in damage-control mode only.

Then, during dessert, Cynthia gave him a Hindu Kara, a closed, circular bracelet. The gift made no sense to Ran because Cynthia knew he never wore jewelry. She knew he didn't like to wear those kinds of things, but there it was.

"It makes you a forever member of our family," she told him.

Cynthia put it on his wrist, kissed him, and smiled. Ran reluctantly went with the flow but quietly acknowledged to himself that the two lovers were way out of sync.

What the hell, she gave it to me, I'll give it a try, he thought. She was noticeably nervous, and he blamed the new conditions she was living under.

The next morning, they had plans to meet at the Saint Coffeeshop near Amsterdam's floating flower market. Ran got to the Bloemenmarkt early, bought some Bird of Paradise seeds, and took a table across the street.

Cynthia arrived late, her hands shaking, reached into her purse, and laid ten pictures of a young girl on the table. She did not say a word. Ran could see the tears rolling down Cynthia's cheeks. For sure, he felt an earthquake of emotions coming on.

He picked up the individual photos one by one as the clunky Kara on his wrist banged against the granite tabletop. He was disliking it more and more. Keeping his head down, he did the math and took a big gulp of air.

He lifted his eyes to meet hers. Cynthia's eyes were covered by her hands, her head was down, and her elbows were on the table.

What does a fifty-one-year-old man say when his lover surprises him with a twelve-year-running secret, a daughter? Obviously, other people knew about her. Cynthia's husband had to know. Ran didn't.

"We have a daughter?" he asked, prompting her to look at him.

Head up, Cynthia nodded. "Yes."

Head down again, Ran arranged them in order of size and turned them to face her.

With their eyes locked again, she said, "Her name is Panita. It means glorious, beautiful girls in Hindi. She will be twelve in January. Your name is on her birth certificate."

Cynthia rewound the film, starting with her recent visit when she told Panita about him.

She added, "She's so excited that you are an American."

Ran did not laugh and felt the earthquake rising to 8.0 on the Richter scale.

Cynthia rationalized her choices, saying that she was not good mother material, that Alamelu was the best mother, and how normal it was in their community for a grandmother to raise her granddaughter.

"Please, Ran, let her grow up in Paramaribo until she is ready to fly on her own," she pleaded.

"It will be sooner than normal since she has our wild genes. She is already a force and quite different from her classmates."

"She knows about you and now you her. It will be easy to welcome each other into your lives. Thank God she's like you, Ran, and not me."

Ran held on for dear life; the tremors were shaking his whole soul. He had heard some of what she had been saying as he recalled the places they had shared when Panita was five, then eight, and so on. And their first rendezvous in Costa Rica after she had given birth, he hadn't picked up any clues then? *Shame on me*, he thought.

"I know you will be cool with our wishes to let her grow up in Suriname. My mother knows I am telling you today and she will tell Panita. Make your calls and go see her," Cynthia urged.

She had been doing all the talking while he was trying to figure out what to say. He felt like he was a collapsing building falling brick by brick.

Collecting himself, he looked her straight in the eye and

asked, "So, our connection as we have known it has changed? The lovemaking rendezvous, the yearning? Cynthia, why didn't you tell me you were . . . ?"

As if choreographed by a maestro, a Dutch diplomatic car pulled up in front of their table and honked. Cynthia got up immediately, kissed Ran's cheek, entered the back of the Mercedes and away it went. He hadn't completed his question.

Ran sat alone at the table for another hour looking at the photos she had left. His heart was heavier than a manhole cover. He thought of the feather on his ass and knew he had a lot of work ahead.

He shook his head in wonder at the twelve-year-old girl, his daughter, Panita. He would have to think about how best to enter his new daughter's life. He thought of his other two daughters and wondered what they'd make of having a half-sister from exotic Suriname.

When the tremors began to recede, he took stock of where he was at the moment. His wild love affair with Cynthia was at an end. The dragon lady he had been warned about long ago had finally struck.

Ran could not bring himself to be angry with her. He didn't try. He was thankful for the years they had together, and that she had given him the gift of Panita. At least she had finally shared that truth.

He got up slowly, walked to the Central Station, jumped on the nearest tram, and rode it round trip for three hours. When he got back to his hotel, he went to bed and stared at the ceiling until he fell asleep. He got up the next morning at dawn with a heavy heart.

Cynthia? She was miserable also. Her driver had dropped her off at Central Station where she caught the train back to her condo in Den Haag. Her twelve-year-old, smelly burden was finally lifted; she cried the night away until there were no more tears left in her body.

It was as if Ran and Cynthia were two ships that collided in the open sea with both ballast tanks pierced and taking on water. The ships would sink or capsize unless the captains took command and made smart, survival decisions. During the next twenty-four hours, both were at their respective helms fighting for their lives and headed in opposite directions.

The reason Ran was in Amsterdam was to begin the next afternoon. He would meet a basketball team at Schiphol Airport and guide them through Amsterdam for two nights, head to Germany, and then finish in Paris. It was good business for his new company and something to take his mind off the previous day's tragedy.

On the bus headed to Paderborn, Germany, he fiddled with the Kara. It was like wearing a tire rim on his wrist. Cynthia had confused him that night at Garoeda and the events of the last three days had doomed any chance of him wearing it.

The team and Ran checked into the Galerie-Hotel in the middle of Paderborn, Germany. It was a charming cross between an art gallery and hotel and the coaches loved it. Not able to sleep, he lay in bed recalling all the time he and Cynthia had spent together and how each occasion lined up with Panita's birthdays.

He got up in the middle of the night, put Panita's pictures in chronological order, checked his passport, and then wrote where they had met during each year. He was disappointed in himself because he hadn't picked up any clues in the twelve years. Cynthia had acted her role very well.

One of their continuing debates had been the nature versus nurture question, always giving examples that supported one of their positions at that time.

He remembered that she had taken a more extreme position on the nature side in the past years. He mostly agreed, but always a bit softer, say 60–40. But the past couple of years, Cynthia had gone more extreme to 90–10 nature. *Had Panita's nature moved her to this position?* he wondered.

Now at 4 a.m. and tired, he took the tire rim off his wrist and threw it out the window of his room.

On his before-coffee walk around the centrum the next morning, he stopped in front of Juweilier Salmen and looked in the window. It was the first time in his life he had ever looked through a jewelry store window.

He saw a bracelet that got his attention. It was a handsome, two-piece clasp with small, twisted cables connecting two gold circles.

He thought, *It is more my style if, in fact, I have one.*

The jewelry store was closed, it was early in the morning, and he decided he would return later to buy it. In the hours after he saw the bracelet in the window, he became consumed with the idea of replacing Cynthia's Kara with a bracelet of his choosing.

When Ran returned to the store in the afternoon, Hans Salmen was sitting at his counter reading a newspaper. Ran pointed to the one he liked in the window and then asked the jeweler about a similar one for his daughter. Hans went to the back room and brought out a smaller and more feminine one. Juweilier Salmen was proud of both.

With a gift for Panita in his pocket, Ran wore his new bracelet across the street and for the rest of his life.

Three weeks later, Ran called the Simonstraat 81 house number after returning from Paris and had a long talk with Alamelu. They agreed that Ran would call Panita the next evening.

The first call with his daughter was awkward, but it was a beginning. It ended with her promising to look up Milwaukee, Wisconsin, where Ran lived.

Father and daughter talked three more times before Ran planned a secret visit to Paramaribo. Each call was easier and more relaxed. Since he had arranged sixteen scholarships for Surinamese athletes in the United States and Cynthia was no longer a resident of Suriname, he felt no fear of returning to Paramaribo, though Bouterse was still in power.

He had arrived on Suriname Airways through Miami. Finding Voss in terrible condition, he moved to the Torarica Hotel. No one knew he was there, including Alamelu. Ran wanted to meet Panita on his terms and in his style. His fantasy was to surprise her coming out of school and for her to recognize him immediately. But first, he wanted to lay his eyes on her without her knowing.

Outside the Saint Louise School in Paramaribo, students' parents were watching an unfamiliar, middle-aged white man standing behind a tree on the campus grounds. The temperature was 93 degrees in the shade and the humidity above 80 percent. The man was wearing a white shirt, but the waiting parents could see he was sweating like hell. They were comfortable in their air-conditioned cars. They knew better than to stand outside. But he didn't.

They started to look at him with suspicion. When their children got in the car, they still kept an eye on the strange man. *He's not one of us*, they decided.

"Did he walk here?" someone asked out loud.

Ran was trying to catch his breath. He was close to hyperventilating. He hadn't been able to find a parking place close enough to the school to see her, so he had to walk twenty minutes to the school's entrance. He wanted only to see her that first day.

When the bell rang, his heart felt like it would jump out of his body and when he tested his voice, it was barely a squeak, like when he first turned the corner and saw Cynthia. Sure, he was having a hard time breathing, but it wasn't the outside weather.

And then out the door, she bounded. He had left the photos of her at home in Milwaukee on purpose. It was easy to recognize Panita, just as Cynthia had told him. She and a friend had turned away from where he was semi-hiding, walked down a few cars, and got in one. The other parents watched him stagger back to his car as they drove by him.

He returned to the Torarica and planned his entry into her life, the next day, a Friday. He would arrive on Mgr. Wulfinghstraat early enough in the afternoon to get a good parking place. He would wait in his rental, air-conditioned car like the rest of the parents and jump out as soon as the bell rang.

First thing that morning, he drove to Simonstraat 81 and knocked on the screen door. Alamelu welcomed him with open arms and immediately dismissed herself to "freshen up." She returned perfectly coiffed and wearing a different dress. She cried as they talked, and it was in these moments that Ran was thankful that Alamelu was Panita's mother.

They reviewed the days of his visit and, more important, acknowledged each of their roles in Panita's life. He thanked her and she apologized for Cynthia's behavior. It was naturally easy for him to accept Alamelu as his daughter's mother. Ran encouraged Alamelu to invite the family and friends to visit while he was at her home.

Before leaving, he excused himself to look out the kitchen window.

Alamelu laughed. "Elvis died some time ago in the tree. We had a hard time getting him untangled. My neighbor wants to put a VACANCY sign on the tree. Ran laughed then too.

That afternoon, the bell rang, and the children began to leave school. Ran was standing in front of the school this time, easily visible.

Panita saw him, stopped, turned away from Asti, and walked straight to him.

"I know who you are," she said, looking him straight in his eyes.

Ran had tears in his eyes.

"Asti, my father, my father!" Panita shouted.

Asti came running toward them. Her mother got out of her car and greeted him. Ran fought back his tears.

"Can I take you home?" he asked Panita.

She nodded eagerly and they walked hand in hand to his car as all the yesterday's parents put two and two together. Panita's American father was in town and the Hindu community was already abuzz.

Panita saw her father wiping away his tears as she got in the car. *Hmm,* she thought, *he's way more emotional than Mata.*

She rolled the window down and yelled out to her friends, "My father picked me up today." Then Panita turned to him and said, "This is the best surprise of my life."

Alamelu prepared a feast of roti chicken and curried vegetables. Uncles, aunts, and cousins streamed in to confirm Ran's existence. Friends brought more food. Father and daughter sat on the couch together greeting the visitors and answering questions. Sometimes Ran would have the answer, sometimes Panita would. Asti came early and left late.

Everyone laughed a lot and rolled their eyes. Ran's and Panita's awkwardness melted away by 11 p.m.; they yawned together and finalized their plans for Saturday.

It was decided that she could invite her best friends to a pool party at the Torarica the next afternoon. He had no idea what to expect but was looking forward to watching and listening to the twelve-year-old Surinamese girls. He figured he could sit on the deck and get up to speed on the conveyor belt headed toward sixteen.

The afternoon culminated with the group chanting, "Show us your tattoo."

The time had come to confirm her mother's story.

"My mother has a tattoo of a feather on her right cheek. I saw it. She told me you had one too. So prove to me and my friends that you really are my father!" Panita shouted like a carnival barker.

Ran seized the moment. He laughed and pretended he didn't know what she was talking about. Still playing his role of ignorance, he pulled down the right side of his suit with his thumb. Nothing.

Panita was having none of it. She quickly put her finger in the left side of his waistband, pulled it down, and the twelve-year-olds screamed. They jockeyed for a better look, then one girl asked if she could touch it. Arm around his waist, his around her shoulders, she monitored the touches. They had great fun.

Much to the chagrin of the nuns, the next week, all of Saint Louise School knew that Panita's mother had a tattoo on her right hip and her father had a tattoo on his left hip. Of course, the feathers got bigger and bigger, as did Panita's brazen reputation in the school.

It was set that she would spend the night with Ran at the Torarica before he departed the next day. Father and daughter now alone, they enjoyed a quiet dinner and made plans on how they would communicate going forward. He wrote down all her friends' names and encouraged her to keep him informed about all the girl drama. Showing a perfect sense of humor, she said, oh so innocently, "Drama? Us? You must be kidding!"

Ran told her that she had two half-sisters in the United States who would be curious to see her pictures and, of course, meet her. They agreed to talk to Alamelu about when Panita could visit him in the States.

Panita asked Ran when she could get her feather tattoo. He laughed and said, "When you are a bit older . . . and Mamalu approves. But don't worry, your mother and I will want you to get one so we can all match."

The chef came out to greet them. By this time everyone in the hotel knew their story, and he served them sweet vanilla custard with a dollop of passion fruit in the middle. Ran couldn't believe it, used his napkin to wipe his eyes, and told Panita how much the fruit meant to him and her mother.

After dessert, he gave her the bracelet, carefully nestled in a German jewelry box. He showed her his bracelet and told her the story of when he bought them.

"From now on, when I touch or look at my bracelet, I will think of this moment with you."

Panita snapped hers on her right wrist and stretched it across the table to touch Ran's. She said, "Me too. Thank you, dad." Ran thought his heart would burst.

Later, they went back to Ran's room and put the photos of her life from birth to eleven years on the floor. Panita lit up the room with her anecdotal stories of life on David Simon-straat 81. Ran loved listening to her voice.

Describing a trip on the Suriname River when she was nine, she fell asleep on the floor in his room.

As he had done so often with her mother, he picked Panita up and carried her to her adjoining room, gently placed her onto the bed, fixed her pillow, covered her, kissed her fore-head, and fell asleep on the floor beside her bed, listening to her breathe.

About the Author

Lee Frederick grew up in the 1950s as a free-range chicken in a rural village, one mile east of the Illinois River. He played basketball well enough in high school to receive a scholarship from Bradley University, where he played on the championship team in the 1964 National Invitational Tournament at Madison Square Garden.

He favored playing in his village over New York City. He says, "Playing in Madison Square Garden lacked the intimacy, emotion, and meaning we felt playing in front of the standing-room-only crowds in our cracker box gym, capacity 320."

Frederick earned a BS and MS in psychology from Bradley University. In between the degrees, he matriculated at sea as a deckhand on the Norwegian ship *MS Santos* on its route down the eastern coasts of North and South America. He worked as a school psychologist in 1968 and then coached basketball at three NCAA universities for eighteen years.

In 1986, Frederick and Duane Woltzen formed Sport Tours International, Inc., in Wisconsin. It was the first company of its kind to arrange international trips for basketball teams and produce tournaments outside the mainland.

Frederick is a lifelong knife sharpener and operates The Sharp Brothers, LLC, with his son, Austin, in Wisconsin and California.

www.ingramcontent.com/pod-product-compliance
Lightning Source LLC
Chambersburg PA
CBHW060456300726
48975CB00008B/2536